Dreaming Out Loud

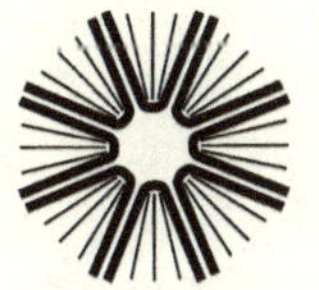

Dreaming Out Loud

LYDIE SALVAYRE

Translated from the French by Alison L. Strayer

GAZEBO BOOKS SUMMER HILL 2025

Gazebo Books
PO Box 375
Summer Hill
New South Wales 2130
Australia
gazebobooks.com.au

Original French edition published by Éditions du Seuil, Paris, France.

National Library of Australia
Cataloguing-in-Publication Entry
Author: Lydie Salvayre
Dreaming Out Loud
ISBN: 978 1 7636009 0 4

Cover and interior design by Mountains Brown Press

Cover and frontispiece image: Alamy Stock Photo

'Every dream is a struggle.'

Victor Hugo
The Promontory of the Dream

1

To Miguel de Cervantes Saavedra

Sir, I'll tell you right away that I'm in no mood for jokes, and the way you treat your Quixote is not to my taste.

You claim that his brain is filled with rubbish he has read in books and believes to be true, which leads him to commit acts of madness.

But is it mad to believe that literature is not a dead letter, a mantelpiece ornament or useless patter, but very much alive, an intimate experience that knocks life sideways?

Is it mad to revolt against the crap we witness every day and fight it with whatever means that come to hand, even at the risk of breaking our necks?

Is it mad to want to be the bulwark and support of the disinherited of all kinds, at the risk of displeasing the *Santa Hermandad*, who make sure that nothing undermines its Most Holy Church and Most Catholic Majesty?

Would you prefer for indifference, resignation and abdication to become our lot, to gaze unflinching at the miseries of others when they do not concern us?

Would you prefer that we denounce them, while taking care not to do the right thing, as our bogus rebels contrive so masterfully to do, with their looks of indignation, trembling voices, and artfully dishevelled attire, to later revel in their very fatal impotence?

Or, worse, would you prefer a world in which no one believes in anything anymore or devotes themselves to anything, and more or less cynically prides themselves on it?

Would you prefer a world in which there is nothing to get excited about, except perhaps the soaring price of Tencent Holdings shares?

A world where enthusiasm, ardour, and imperious, wild desire would only be inflamed by the prospect of reaping ever-rising dividends?

Forgive me, sir, for addressing you in the words of the times in which I live, but your book brings me back to the present with such fury that I forget that four centuries stand between us.

A new reproach springs to my mind at this moment. Tell me, sir, why you so make fun of your Quixote for not adapting to that which people, to save time, call reality?

Is it mad to rebel against this flat, meagre, piteous reality (or which at least presents itself as such) and prefer the one we have inside, so much vaster and more desirable?

Don't you think that the reality we perceive with our inner eye from the depths of our private forests and enchanted Indies, Blessed Islands and gardens of memory, don't you think that this reality gives the other one (whose shape is determined by consensus) a rare colour and zest?

Sir, do not misunderstand my meaning. I am not saying that Don Quixote seeks to foist upon us a specious illusion in place of reality, as a few inattentive readers have asserted; or, to put it another way, to substitute his own little subjective vision for another that is supposedly objective – and horribly rectangular.

What I am saying, sir, is that Quixote perceives reality perfectly well, but that he perceives it from what Victor Hugo calls the promontory of the dream. And from this promontory, which transports him to the ends of the visible world, the reality he discovers suddenly acquires a new dimension. It transmutes, expands, unfurls, bursts its boundaries and sometimes takes on aspects of the fantastic.

In other words, Quixote can see what most of us do not. He can peer into obscurity, discover abysses where others only see their feet, see horror where others see nothing but meaningless platitudes, and in some faces recognise a splendour most of us are too blind to see.

He sees more. He sees big. He sees in another way.

He sees everything which reality lacks.

He sees the way a poet does, dear sir, and views the world in a way that is anything but bovine.

He sees that which is not apparent or cannot be imagined. He sees the abnormal in the normal with a rare acuity.

He perceives everything as a novelty, and can therefore grasp the strangeness of objects which our habits make familiar, discover extraordinary facets of the most obtuse forms, discern the most surprising similarities between them, feel the closest affinity with the ones most unattainable and the greatest distance from those within reach and behold the world with that sense of strangeness which sometimes overwhelms us but is ground underfoot by our routines with great blows of the heel. From the promontory of his dreams, things and men are bathed in quite a different light. His vision somehow corrects the myopia we are subject to when seeing them only in the light of our cold dry reason.

Is that what you call his madness, sir?

And if that is so, do you wish for a life depleted of its dreams and utopias, entirely given over to useful morals?

Would you like us to abandon everything that has for all of time kept women and men on their feet, the appetite for dreams, the love of risk, the thirst for new things, whatever name you give them?

Might you have forgotten that Utopia is one of life's greatest helpers?

Might you have forgotten that it infuses life with the necessary impetus to move forward in the darkest night, break through the walls of the Unknown, knock them down, go beyond them, and open itself to unknown languages, unimagined horizons, new Americas?

Might you have forgotten that Utopia constitutes an extraordinary incentive for thought, which it pushes towards unspoilt or fallow lands, waiting for it to give substance to inconceivable hypotheses? Are you not aware that the most beautiful discoveries are born of this kind of exploration of the impossible in which a few quixotic spirits have engaged?

And that the most outrageous utopias are destined to come true one day, all of History has taught us that, dear sir.

Do you want to deprive us of them by discrediting them, as cynical proponents of realpolitik strive to do today, turning a blind eye to a mountain of crap so as better to reap profit from the world as it is?

Moreover, Utopia is a word these gentlemen are careful to avoid, or which they only use with the most extreme circumspection, always in order to disqualify it (they would say: *demonetise* it), and relegate its use to daydreamers in robes and slippers whom they know to be as harmless as houseflies flicked away with the back of the hand.

These gentlemen, of a species I don't believe is soon to be extinct, who work tirelessly to build their power, prefer not to use this disturbing word which – startlingly – they associate with the flames of desire, the upheaval of spirits and great revolutionary fervour: all things which they fear almost as much as they do their own ruin.

What I fear, sir, is that the shortage of utopias among those who govern us, and want more than anything to be realistic, will back us into the worst kind of corner if no new Don Quixote comes crashing into the landscape.

I leave you with these worried remarks, whose cause you cannot understand. I will resume this letter when I've regained some measure of calm.

2

A night has passed, dear sir, and I'm still in no mood for jokes because your stubborn insistence on mistreating your hidalgo frankly infuriates me. You plant a barber's basin on his head for a helmet. You fit him out with patched-together breeches, arm him with a rust-eaten lance and a tree branch for a halberd. You sit him on a spavined nag, judiciously called Rocinante. In short, you make him look like a poor scarecrow, clattering from head to toe with scrap metal.

By making him a laughing stock in this way, you license those who fancy themselves as connoisseurs of culture to laugh until they drop at the mention of the ridiculous jumping jack who by dint of an exacerbated idealism, mistakes quite innocuous windmills for fearsome giants.

A little clarification, here, to silence those benighted ninnies once and for all: at Quixote's time, windmills were a novelty, and nothing was more natural than to find them disconcerting and fantastic, to misunderstand their function. Just as it is natural for us today to be bewildered by the technological innovations which overwhelm us and we are far from mastering; I speak from experience. This is the speed at which the world evolves and casts us off, today as yesterday; it is the same resistance aroused in us – rightly or wrongly – by these too-rapid developments, which Quixote comes to challenge in his own way.

It seems to me, moreover, that the authors of the chivalric romances whom Quixote admired were so busy extoling the virtues of their incomparable champions that they neglected to specify what kind of giants they were up against. Winged? Aggressive? In combat with the gods? The rivals of men?

So as I was saying, you never miss a chance to make your Quixote appear grotesque and pronounce him mad, when others would simply declare him a poet, philosopher or genius.

Here, if we may, sir, let us return a moment to your judgement, both hasty and flippant, with respect to his madness.

I grant you that your Quixote is mad, if it is mad to be generous in a world which never gives anything without a promise of return, a world bereft of love and mercy, and even shorter on pity (a kind of madness which, I agree, not just anyone can achieve).

I grant you that he is mad if it is mad to choose to live according to that which your heart and soul decree.

I grant you he is mad, if madness is the name one gives to whatever visionary power continues to survive in a being.

I grant you that he is mad, if the madman is he who has preferred to go mad, in the socially accepted sense of the word, rather than be false to a certain superior idea of human honour. This, Antonin Artaud's definition, fits Quixote like a glove; he cannot help but rise up against injustice because, as he declares, his knightly honour depends on it.

I grant you that he is mad if you conceive of madness in the manner of Nietzsche, as the mask that hides a knowledge that is fatal and too certain, and the ultimate recourse of superior men to whom only two exits are offered: going mad, or pretending to be mad, at the risk of getting caught up in the game, and sometimes getting lost in it.

I grant you he is mad, if you consider *Les Chants de Maldoror* and their divine poison to be the work of a lunatic, victim of the treponema, as he was bad-mouthed by two or three pedants of his time, hack writers of rancid soul who didn't hold a candle to him.

Please forgive me, sir, for bringing up the names Artaud, Nietzsche, Lautréamont, which you can't possibly know. I keep forgetting that you are from another time.

I grant you that he is mad if he is mad in the eyes of those who tolerate no singularity or misconduct, who burn human beings at the stake in public squares for having turned their backs on the rules laid down by your Most Holy Church.

And who, in any case, dear sir, holds the truth about madness? Who decides who is mad and who is not? Certainly not the Church, nor the State, nor their police brigades – nor their psychiatrists, come to that.

It suddenly occurs to me that the latter did not exist in your time, for madness was not, then, considered a curable disease but the disturbance of a soul that has splintered beneath the blows of God's will, or that of Satan.

Psychiatrists (whom I spent a lot of time with when I practised the profession myself), psychiatrists, since then, have prospered, never hesitating to lend their know-how to the worst kind of undertakings, and in numerous subjects, causing more harm than good. We know, for example, that the carpenter Zimmer, who took the poet Hölderlin into his home, was a thousand times more understanding and a thousand times less brutal than Doctor Johann Heinrich Ferdinand von Autenrieth, who treated the poet so well in his clinic in Tübingen that he emerged completely shattered. We also know that Doctor Beer, who poked around the soul of poor Van Gogh, reducing it to pulp with his 'shitty scalpel', saw him as nothing more than a degenerate type of schizophrenic, heedless of material life and incapable of supervising his interests to make his business prosper (these are the exact terms of his psychiatric report); all this for having made the mistake of going off to paint at night by the light of candles he had fixed to his hat so as to better contemplate the beauty of the landscape.

Finally, I grant you that he is mad if preventing violence from being inflicted on the most vulnerable, and defending a valet against the brutality of his boss to you comes down to plain and simple lunacy.

To compel you, sir, to change your outlook on your creature, allow me to remind you of the episode to which I have just alluded: Don Quixote is riding in the La Mancha countryside, you write, when he hearkens to the plaintive cries of someone in distress. He turns around and, without a second thought, rushes to the place from where the cries seemed to proceed.

He then discovers a young shepherd, naked from the waist up, tied to an oak tree, being flogged by a lusty peasant with great lashes of a belt.

Now, any attack on the dignity of men, any treatment that lowers and humiliates, any violence that breaks bodies and souls, revolts our Quixote and makes him quake with anger.

Shameless man, he says to the peasant, by what right do you attack a helpless unfortunate?

The peasant, taken aback at the sight of this great armoured beanpole (and understandably so!), replies that he is punishing his valet for negligence and having the audacity to ask for his wages.

But Quixote is organically, biologically, viscerally incapable of allowing injustice to be done, and before the reasons invoked by the peasant, his blood boils. Purple with rage, he orders the peasant, in a tone that brooks no dissent, to untie his valet on the double and pay him within the hour if he does not want to end up impaled upon a lance. Quixote does not go in for half measures.

Dumbfounded, the peasant complies. But he can't help quibbling, and offers to deduct from the wages due the price of the shoes he provided for the valet as well as the price of the bloodletting performed when he was sick.

Quixote's astounding reply, worthy of a Marxist thinker: *For all that he has damaged the leather of your shoes, you have damaged the skin of his body; and if the barber drew blood from him when he was ill, you have drawn blood from him when he was well. So he owes you nothing.*

Sir, have you taken a good look at what you wrote?

In 1604, your Quixote becomes enraged at those who exploit the strength of others and use them up, suck their blood, exhaust them for their personal gain.

And that the peasant in question takes advantage of his status as boss to assume the right to punish his valet as he sees fit, such as screwing him over with complete impunity (could this be a definition of management?) does not impress Quixote one bit. It only makes him angrier.

Marxist, I tell you! Centuries before the industrial revolution, before assembly lines and their infernal rhythms which would exhaust the bodies and minds of factory workers. Centuries before Chaplin's

Modern Times and the writings of Simone Weil, who will tell us about the banal horror of it all.

The matter apparently resolved, Quixote rides away and vanishes into the forest.

But no sooner has he left than the peasant, who no doubt thinks himself a good Christian (he's never missed a mass) but who has privileges to defend and a humiliation to avenge, Christianly abandons the promise he made Don Quixote, Christianly seizes his valet by the arm and ties him to the oak tree, and deals him so many Christianly blows that the young man is left more flayed and bloodied than Saint Bartholomew. Such is the prevailing morality in the Spain of Felipe II, which Don Quixote brings to light.

Through this kind of intervention, sir, your hidalgo not only corrects an abuse of authority which contravenes – surely you agree – the teachings of the Gospel, but exposes the kind of logic that makes the peasant landowner believe that his is the only law and that he has every right to brutalise his subordinate and, moreover, gouge him. In short: the reasoning of the affluent is the one which always prevails.

Is this what you call madness, sir, denouncing injustice and defending those who are its victims?

To demonstrate that your creature is far from being as mad as you pretend to believe and make us believe, but instead acts in the noblest and most reasonable way possible, I present a second example from the pages of your book. You write: one morning Don Quixote meets a column of galley slaves (whom I imagine resembling George Clooney, John Turturro and John Goodman in *O Brother, Where Art Thou?* with balls and chains on their feet, and pink and white striped tunics, but certainly far less dashing, less glamorous and far less sexy than the three I have just named, and – to spare no detail – in very sorry state), a column of galley slaves supervised by the wardens of the *Santa Hermandad*, on their way to who-knows-what port to serve as rowers in the galleys of the king.

Quixote's heart abruptly sinks at the sight of these chained men whom he calls his brothers, and immediately thinks of helping them.

Indeed, he believes that he has every right to do so. A knight-errant worthy of his title does not have to check whether the chained men or any of the suffering people he meets along his way are innocent or guilty of their misfortunes.

A knight-errant is by no means a priest, a politician, or a prosecutor, all of whom are able to decide who is good and who is bad (but good or bad in whose eyes, for what reason, from what point of view, or in terms of what interests?).

A knight-errant by no means has the soul of a magistrate, not by a long shot. He draws up no indictment and he does not judge, because the life that God has given men and women is not to be judged.

He simply does not consider it right that honest men should be instruments of punishment to others; these are the words you make Quixote utter. And he wants to take what is unjust and replace it with the just. That is all. And that is immense.

So Quixote, as a perfect gentleman (forgive me, as a perfect hidalgo), courteously entreats the guards of the *Santa Hermandad* to release these unfortunate men.

Big mistake! It is common knowledge that those of mediocre soul understand nothing but barked commands and the vociferations of brutes.

Sensing they are unreceptive to his philanthropic notions, and disinclined to embark on a thorough discussion of the question of evil in Plotinus, Quixote tries nonetheless to convince them that it is monstrous to enslave men whom God and Nature have created free and to deprive them of movement.

The guards listen to the speech, exchanging vague looks of commiseration before the crackpot-at-arms who delivers it. Observing this, Quixote loses his temper, as he often does, prone as he is to fits of pique. He fulminates against these hearts of stone, shudders from head to toe; his face contorts with fury, and all of a sudden, digging his heels into Rocinante's sides, he charges the archers (whom today we would call the representatives of Law Enforcement) and tries to knock them senseless with great blows of his rapier.

Not for a moment does he think of the risk of reprisals he incurs (and these, indeed, will not be long in coming).

Faced with this abrupt turnaround, the galley slaves are stunned, so outlandish, extraordinary, unimaginable does the thing seem to them, so immense the gap between the conduct of this fanatic and the prevailing mores of the National-Catholic powers, so brutally has he broken with the edicts of holy custom.

Then, their stupefaction having faded, the magnanimity of such behaviour seems to them so inadmissible that they infer it is the product of madness or holiness (the two are so close), or idiocy (I remind you in passing – though you already know – that the word 'idiot' comes from the Greek meaning 'singular').

From there to considering they can violently reject the extravagant knight who freed them, and, with no risk to themselves, brutalise something which they take to be weakness, is just one little step. They take the step.

Freed from their chains and realising that Don Quixote is alone and defenceless (they won't be daunted by the likes of Sancho!), they quickly guess that this character who possessed the insane courage to attack the Most Holy and Most Untouchable *Hermandad* is clearly a being who inspires not so much terror as mockery, a vulnerable being, easily broken.

And so they jump at the chance to avenge themselves for their misery and servitude, taking it out on Quixote, just as other men, to avenge themselves for their sorry fates, lash out at their dog, their wife, their children or their crockery.

Taking his courage as a personal affront, with consummate zeal they pull him from his mount, throw him to the ground, beat him black and blue, pelt him with a torrent of pebbles and strip him of his breeches, leaving him bare-arsed (you have him appear in his birthday suit a number of times in your novel – I prefer to abstain, dear sir, from interpreting this kind of obsession, lest I offend you) and take to their heels forthwith.

This brings me to a painful question, sir, one which has tormented me for a long time: Why do gestures of a certain nobility call forth so much hatred?

Are the mediocre such cowards that they do not forgive those who act in an edifying manner?

Do they punish them for behaviour whose high-mindedness reveals their own pettiness and meanness of spirit?

Do they hate them for being what they will never be?

Do they think that an act of generosity is the sign of a flaccid soul, the proof of an unmanly, delicate, romantic nature; literate, with a penchant for unreality; in short a feminine nature, which explains the barrage of blows which logically ensue?

Or do they take their own indignity for an indisputable superiority? It is a relatively common position in the times in which we live, and comes to the fore with uncommon vigour at the time of our presidential elections. You don't know what presidential elections are? A contest of promises, dear sir, organised to give people the illusion that they can choose their king.

The fact is that without being aware of it, these wretches (I am talking about the galley slaves who beat Quixote to avenge themselves for their own weakness) reproduce power relations which are deeply entrenched in them but of which they are themselves the victims. These relations are all they have known and seem to them as incontestable as the laws of nature; they want nothing more than to perpetuate them, sometimes with a ferocity proportional to their degree of subjugation.

Such is the terrible conclusion you draw.

Allow me to tell you, sir, that now, four centuries later, things have changed very little, though they have taken on forms that are more insidious and of smooth appearance, so smooth in fact that they are now almost sure of winning; I mean, of leading us to disaster.

Every day we see the most destitute populations lend their support to authoritarian powers which, by inundating them with demagogic fables and speeches designed to stir up fear, exploit and lead them to demand the very things which subjugate and turn them into commodities.

Convinced that souls can be kneaded like bread and made to believe any old bill of goods, they pass off their decrees that are disgusting in the extreme as politics.

Come back my Quixote!

Come back soon, before it's too late.

3

Everyone today, dear sir, knows the tale of the brave Knight of the Rueful Countenance. In the 1600s, a little middle-aged hidalgo, a bachelor living modestly from his lands (four acres to be precise) with his niece and a housekeeper, feels such passion for novels of chivalry and the feats of the heroes who have stoked his dreams, that one fine day he decides to leave everything to follow their example.

From that day on, he will put his dreams to the test.

He will give them substance.

He will conduct himself in such a way as to verify whether the sublime virtues of the characters of the novels he loves are not (to use his own expression) like faith without deeds: full of hot air!

If the beauty, honour and courage praised in literature cannot be found in the acts of everyday but are mere formalities, lyric-poetical verbiage, in flagrant contradiction with the deeds of ordinary life, what then is the point of books?

Quixote will take the plunge. He will tear himself away from his library full of novels in which everything is wondrous: springs are pure, swords are made of emerald, captive princesses ravishing, their rescuers heroic with never a hair out of place, skies are azurean and dawns always rosy.

And he will finally Live – do the thing called Living.

He will face the world head on, grapple with it, press it to his heart, taste it, touch it, breathe it in, feel the throb of its pulse. He will cling to it, rub himself against it, immerse himself in it, and sometimes wallow, risk his hide there, seize it with all the uncertainty and peril that this implies, and then, at other times, rush at it, all nerves and muscles tensed, bite and attack it, if at any time it flouts his principles. He will plunge into the human throng with his entire spirit, his entire sensibility. He will commingle with the living – all kinds of living beings, shepherds, muleteers, ploughmen, innkeepers, dukes and duchesses, duennas, peasant women, and maybe, with a little luck, fearsome monsters.

Starting today, that is what he hungers for.

If ink has killed words by riveting them to the page, may the text return to its deathly immobility!

And may the inattentive reader be disabused. No, no, a thousand times no, Quixote is no idle dreamer, fantasist, or bookworm with his head in the clouds, as some careless commentators see him. This fallacy has been sustained quite long enough! He is by no means the birdbrain, crackpot, and stranger to the real world – or worse, a cross between a compulsive liar and a shit disturber, to which he has been reduced by those of indolent mind. No, no, a thousand times no!

He'll make his utopia a reality, make the counter-world for which he hopes and prays exist in a present that is instantly present, without postponing to a future time that which he considers his earthly vocation.

He will commit himself wholeheartedly to the task to which he believes he has been called and whose achievement is long overdue.

And this commitment will be a dizzying leap for him, a radical break.

From this day on, the literature that was his passion, offering him an ideal world free of nettles, free of flaws, ugliness and heaviness, but cruelly devoid of human presence and the living matter of words, of ineffable things – the grain of a voice, the beauty of a gaze, the geography of wrinkles on a face, from now on, this literature will cease to be a dead letter.

No longer will it moulder on shelves grown too narrow to hold his dreams and which the sunlight scarcely reaches.

And into life he will carry this literature he has read so voraciously. He will cast it into the open air, shake it up and dust it off.

He will get it dirty.

And may it live – God, may it live and get drunk on air! May it fill both hands to overflowing with reality! And may the body of the text become embedded in the body of flesh, make it tremble, make it blanch, take it to the heights of pleasure! May the two fall into each other's arms! And may the joys and sorrows begin!

There is no poetry other than real action, wrote the insolent Pier Paolo Pasolini in his book *Who is Me.* You don't know who this man is? A poet, writer, filmmaker, assassinated on a beach in Italy in 1975, whose works of rage continue to cry out to me. He was a Don Quixote, in his way. But let us return to the one and only, the original Quixote. Yours, sir.

Your Quixote, who resolved to throw himself, body and dreams, into the world, hoping in that way to make the fictional works so rapturously read become reality.

Dreams, as we have known since Sigmund Freud (another name unknown to you, obviously; but I ask you, sir, to try and endure not knowing everything), dreams cleverly evade the censors: therein lies their intelligence.

Dreams are unusable, idle, and as pointless as the lilies of the field: therein lies their beauty.

A dream, like love, remains a mystery, no matter what lengths we go to in order to unravel it – that is why it is such a fertile source for art. Dreams flow through us like a secret spring that nourishes our soil, and no one at the surface can guess the cause of such abundance.

Quixote will transplant his free, useless, mysterious and fluid dream onto a concrete, brutal, cramped, perfectly calibrated, and often detestable reality.

He will take the risk of enlarging reality to the dimensions of his dream, even if it means damaging, draining, tarnishing his dream a little, reducing it to triviality. He will dream on his feet.

In other words, he will try to realise that goal which most of us strive for. He will hybridise, adjust, or at the very least, attempt to unite dream and reality.

Which, pessimists say, is tantamount to covering latrines in lapis-lazuli.

And which, optimists say, means generating (at last!) the alchemy of which we have for so long been bereft.

Because, if one is to believe Gilles Deleuze (a French philosopher born long after you, sir, of whom I am particularly fond), bourgeois stupidity has put an end to the precious union between thought and action, between the work of the spirit and work of the body, so that, he ruefully says, at present, we can no longer imagine such a thing existing. So that all we have left is the tragic alternative of lives too quiet and orderly for thinkers, or thoughts too wild for living beings.

For a long time now, Western thinkers have ceased to get their hands and bodies dirty.

For a long time now, spiritual life has been promoted at the expense of the physical, judged coarse, imperfect, and perishable as our bones; we turn away from it in disgust to leap into the pure sky of abstractions – a clear, limpid sky, perfectly preserved from the dirty rotten weather of the real.

For a long time, the life of the soul has been judged superior to that of the body. The proof is in the French expression *aller de corps,* 'go from the body', which means to shit.

For a long time, the gulf between what we live each day and what we devise in our heads has widened to the point of becoming an abyss, although some have desperately tried to defy it; some like Antonin Artaud have tried with all their poor might to refuse a divorce of this nature:

'I cannot conceive any work of art as having a separate existence from life itself… I would like to write a Book which would drive men mad, which would be like an open door leading them where they would never have consented to go, in short, a door that opens onto reality.'

Quixote will try to open this door that opens onto a reality he has forsaken for too long.

And so, as of now, he will no longer hover on the threshold of the world.

As of now, he will no longer be shielded from its threats, its suffering, hideousness and wounds, or its joys so powerful they provoke terror.

He will go towards himself.

He will inhabit the world, in the fullest sense of the word.

And this world he will inhabit, and for which he will fight, will be a living world of the here and now, and not a simulacrum made of paper criss-crossed by evanescent shadows. It is a tangible, concrete, rough-edged world, probably cruel and imperfect, warped and disappointing, but filled with men and women made of flesh and dreams, not misty creatures who vanish into space the moment the dream ends.

Quixote will fight for this living world because he feels a deep desire, a fierce and urgent desire to achieve something great, something with panache, bold and heroic, something exemplary which will leave an indelible mark on history, and thanks to which he will be able to look himself in the face and continue to do so for the rest of his days.

So that is how it is. From now on he will live on a human scale, on the same level as other human beings.

The artificial life is over now – the borrowed life with all its false promises.

No more vicarious adventures.

No more praiseworthy intentions one proclaims after dinner, sipping a liqueur, knowing there's no danger of having to put them into action. Gone are the rants with no strings attached, exaltations uttered in dressing gowns and slippers, cushy fantasies, grand and vital sentiments, generally gassy and thus explosive.

No more idle flipping through the pages of the world.

The beautiful dreamer who had infinity for a pillow will take on the full weight of reality and feel it in his body and soul.

In this way, incidentally, he reminds us that the computerised machines which today fill our lives to bursting (dear sir, you could absolutely not imagine these machines, to which we have in a sense become appended like artificial limbs) separate us more each day from the physical, carnal, sensitive experience of others' presence and the world into which your hidalgo is about to venture forth.

Quixote will exist at last! Truly exist, confront, collide with the living world, get hurt, commit himself to this bitch of a life that sometimes does us as much harm as good. No one who does this can escape mishaps and pain – you, of all people, know this.

In another letter, I'll talk about the pain you wickedly make your Quixote endure.

4

I re-read part of your book last night, sir, and I'm sorry to say, my anger at you has gone up a notch instead of diminishing.

Not content with making your Quixote look ridiculous, you make sure that he is beaten, crushed, flattened, stunned, thrashed, poked full of holes, sliced from ear to ear, ridiculed, and showered with stones. You have him torn limb from limb, lynched, booed at, his soul spat upon, his teeth shattered. You have him tormented and violated in thirty-six thousand ways, the better to rub his nose in reality, and *teach him a thing or two*, as those of vulgar mind like to say.

In a word, sir, you martyrise him.

With cruel satisfaction you knock him off his horse more times than can be counted. While you're at it, you have him trampled by a herd of wild bulls. You throw a cat in his face which tears his nose to shreds; you leave him hanging from a window by one arm, and – to cut him down yet another notch – you crown him with a helmet full of cheese (hidden there by Sancho), so the curds drip down his face.

Sir, you seem to take pleasure in hurting him. It is sheer sadism, and I'm not the only one to think so. Believe me, it does not amuse me one little bit.

Why is the fate you devise for him so unremittingly cruel?

What could he have possibly done for you to punish him in this way?

What are you trying to make him pay for?

Are you hoping he will die so you can wash your hands of a book you've grown tired of writing?

Or do you wish to discourage people who continue to hope that there are exceptions to the rule of crushing oppression, singular personalities who possess the courage and the freedom of spirit to tear a hole in the wall of the state-run dungeon where truth suffocates to death?

Do you want to muzzle everyone whose words and deeds seem out of line because they contradict your indisputable logic, just as they take issue with the people who make and break opinion?

Is it your way of whispering, 'This is the price you'll pay for speaking out in any way whatsoever! Try harder to be a spineless yellow-belly. And it's time you adapted to the world as it is!'

Are you, by any chance, one of those people (every era has them) who punish dreamers for dreaming of a here-and-now that differs from the one to which – alas! – the majority is resigned?

Are you, by any chance, one of those people who use different kinds of weapons – swords, fear mongering, advertising, psychiatric diagnoses or politico-economic-religious insinuations – to bring to heel all those who deviate from the roads most travelled?

Or do you believe that this dreadful violence which you force Quixote to endure, page after page, actually possesses an astonishing ability to bring your readers delight? Forgive me, sir, but I cannot help but repeat that the violence you inflict is in no way funny. Grant me the freedom to inform you that it is simply hateful and dismays me no end.

At this very moment, a psychoanalyst friend of mine murmurs in my ear: serious clinical studies reveal that physical and moral harm of one's fellows is a source of pleasure for a great number of subjects. He adds: the spectacle of suffering affords the same people a form of dark delight that is much appreciated. Which explains the success of the crucified Christ with the suggestive little loincloth draped over the willy (a very human willy, indeed), or adventure series such as *Koh-Lanta* or *Fort Boyard* whose audiences are proportional to the cruelty of the abuse inflicted upon their contestants; but that, you cannot understand.

I will grant you, sir, that the context in which you lived would hardly predispose a person to tenderness.

In your era, every celebration was redolent of blood, every execution a form of entertainment.

Starting in 1478, the Inquisition practised banishment and imprisonment, and, with no moderation, execution, torture and burning at the stake.

The Inquisition made man-hunting its great national safari, chasing down all those who aroused suspicion (and they were numerous): new Christians, Protestants, perjurers, pederasts, non-believers, apostates, *alumbrados* (visionaries, crackpots), blasphemers, infidels, fornicators, voluptuaries, the depraved, idol worshippers, the brazen, the lapsed and relapsed, bigamists, insincere Catholics, witches worshiping the Great Goat, abject sodomites, the mentally ill possessed by the devil, all people of low morals, all infernal spirits and incarnations of the Evil One, from whom the All Pure Spain had to be pitilessly cleansed.

The Inquisition was a great silencer while encouraging the most abominable denunciations of unbelievers: god-killing Jews, hypocritically converted; fanatics of the Mohammedan sect. And these denunciations, presented as patriotic duty, engendered a nation of snitches and spies:

instruments of divine will, need we add.

The Inquisition was so powerful that it defied civil justice with impunity, for the greatest good of its Most Holy Church, attracting the assistance of all those who feared and dreamed of belonging to it; for some this belonging was their highest ambition.

By way of punishment, it could go as far as confiscating, in good faith, the fortune of those whom it suspected, an extremely motivating argument which gave people ideas, as the expression goes.

Very creative and inspired in its macabre projects, the Inquisition obliged suspects to wear a tunic called a *sambenito* on which their name and nature of their crime were inscribed. These were tunics of infamy which, at the death of the culprits, had to be exposed in churches to remind the general population of the proscribed family names and thus maintain, over generations, the memory of opprobrium. As a form of ignominy, it was hard to beat.

Every work, you know, bears the date of its creation – is the offspring of its era. The same goes for the meaning it is given, which fluctuates, brightens or darkens, fades or moves into sharper focus – in short, it is constantly recreated with the spirit of the times and the prevailing biases. But whatever the case, sir, the context in which you conceived your work, of which we must, of course, take account, and despite the extenuating circumstances that it seems fair to grant you, I regret to say, if you wanted to give readers a pitiful Quixote, well, sir, you have failed! Your Quixote is quite simply moving. His frailty in this world of brutes can only touch our hearts, while inciting us to reflect on the reasons for the violence he is forced to endure.

You wanted to discredit his actions? Failed again! Because what we remember of these is the inflexible, outrageous and tireless force of insurrection behind them.

What does it matter to Quixote that he is trodden upon like grapes from the vine, or beaten to a pulp? What does it matter to him if he is mocked, duped, or declared insane? And what does it matter that he is the object of the coarsest form of misunderstanding (he does not complain about it, ever, and does nothing to be understood; sometimes he even seems not to care that he is misunderstood).

Nothing fazes or discourages him, and his determination does not weaken by a millimetre.

A gang of boors knock him down? Our Quixote, though pulverised and bloody, dazed and caked with mud, picks himself up, gathers his eclectic paraphernalia, and clanking like a battery of saucepans (my description), painfully gets back on his nag.

Though aching from head to foot, he returns to battle with what remains of his strength, unshakeable and faithful to the pact he has made with himself, that senseless imperative, incomprehensible to anyone but himself, viewed by others as a form of insanity, and yet without which life for him is not worth living. If this imperative did not exist in certain people, sir, would there be artists? Would there be poets? Would there be inventors of genius? Would there be immortal masterpieces? Would your contemporary El Greco have painted *The Martyrdom of Saint Maurice*? Would you have written *Don Quixote of La Mancha*?

But I am getting carried away, sir. I have a certain propensity for doing so.

As I was saying, he returns to battle with the last of his strength, because fighting, he assures us, is a kind of rest for him, but above all because he feels he must, according to his imperious will to improve the world, a will that nothing and nobody can influence.

And though his body is bruised, his soul stands firm, rises up against defeat and resignation, remains straight as an arrow. Therefore he can tell himself with legitimate satisfaction: *Even if he did not accomplish great things, he died trying.*

Quixote never surrenders, because only death can extinguish the passion that burns in him. I understand that this posture may seem exaggerated, grandiloquent and irrelevant to those who will never know this fire of passion. To these faint-hearted beings, these timorous souls, I express my sincere compassion.

A group of muleteers have beat him black and blue? Up he gets and returns to battle, panting, stunned, shattered, but back in the saddle, fired up again and quivering with passionate enthusiasm. Because Quixote is thick-skinned. Because he is full of verve, literary verve, that is. Because he is obstinate. Hard-headed. Like my mother. He is not Spanish for nothing, not the kind to throw in the towel – he's no quitter.

Resignation? He's never heard of it.

So Quixote gets up, gingerly feeling his buttocks. He collects his gear with a clatter, and then performs the ritual gestures that give one courage, the lofty gestures of a mysterious liturgy of war, which I imagine as similar to the ones we see in Rohmer's film *Perceval le Gallois*. With papal gravity, he kisses his buckler, repositions his helmet (equipped with a pasteboard visor), and with a majestic hand seizes his lance (completely corroded by rust), and with the other grasps his shield (in equally bad shape), slips on his gorget (musty and too tight), adjusts his corselet (threadbare), polishes his breastplate (grey with dust and sweat), pronounces a portentous sentence (despite his broken teeth), then with great dignity swings his leg over his mount.

And fie on evil-doers who abuse the weak!

Quixote returns to battle without getting mired in infinite deliberations about the motives of his actions, or endlessly weighing all the pros and cons that could slow him down and prevent him from acting at all.

Picasso said he thought with his eyes. Quixote thinks with his body, with his heart and nerves, and doesn't meditate at every step of the way about what drives him.

No preconceived ideas. No anticipation. No doctrine. No system. No interpretations such as mumdad-oedipus-castration-incest. He goes to battle without any whys or becauses.

The whys, like the becauses, tend to keep experience at arm's length. Moreover, it seems that is their purpose.

But it is precisely in order to resist the allure of these dressing gown-and-slipper tribulations that Quixote got out of his chair, and painfully, courageously, and entirely to his credit left his library, thus breaking with everything that had been his life until that time.

Now he explores, discovers, experiences everything while taking care not to construct subtle and intelligent alibis that could lead him to change his mind, become discouraged or resigned, or to run away.

And he throws himself into action the way one throws oneself into water, alone, head first, with nothing between himself and danger, armed with an iron will and infallible courage, the kind of courage that lies halfway between the extremes of vice that are cowardice and rashness (those are his words); the kind of courage which is always a leap into the unknown and always a beginning, Jankélévitch tells us; always a heads-or-tails wager, he also says; the kind of courage that does not look right or left, or behind, but straight ahead without hedging or retreating, without evasions, and risks everything for all of life; that courage without which the other virtues would be nothing but pipe dreams, without which they could only abort or remain powerless (what would Quixote's sense of justice be worth without his courage to translate it into action?); the courage that is the very condition, the very gesture of freedom.

Whence come the aphorisms I present to you here because to my ears they sound quixotic and may be to your liking:

The first: Without freedom, there can be no literature.

The second: Without courage there can be no freedom.

And this third one, which flows from the other two: Without courage, there can be no writers. Of this, dear sir, I am quite sure. Indeed, it is one of the few things in this world of which I'm really sure.

Quixote returns to battle bravely and without the consent of any power, without accreditation, guardianship, or authorisation, without any sponsor.

Pitted against the actions of his heart and the court of his conscience, these authorities are weightless for him. He ignores them, sovereignly ignores them. Or distrusts them as he does all the machines of power, particularly those which, at his time of history, are the most irrefutable: the Church, the King and Justice.

Never, in any case, does he claim to follow any of them. Never does he brandish their emblem for the purpose of justifying his acts. He never wears their insignia. Everything happens as if these powers had no hold over him, as if they were absolutely foreign to a certain idea he has of greatness.

An anarchist: that's what he is, I am telling you.

An anarchist to the core.

I know that term was not used in your time, and in ours is often pronounced with a certain contempt.

What I seek to convey by using this word is

that Quixote is in no way impressed by those who represent temporal authority, who serve it blindly and wear its uniform: beadles, archbishops, deacons, canons, archers of the *Santa Hermandad* and all the Spanish petty clergy. How can anyone be impressed by a suit? A suit can be thrown out, seems to me. And once it is discarded, who can tell wise from foolish or rich from poor?

The same thing happens in the comedy of this world (as in theatre), *where some play emperors, others popes… But when it is over, that is to say when life ends, death strips them all of the garments that distinguish one from the other, and all are equal in the grave.* These are the words of Quixote.

Here, dear sir, is a little illustration of his libertarian inclinations which I allow myself to put before you.

When Quixote comes face to face, for the second time, with the *argousins* of the *Santa Hermandad*, one of whom brandishes the arrest warrant that has been taken out against him on the very serious grounds that he freed the galley slaves (a gesture that would be qualified today as complicity: 'Accomplice shall mean any person who wittingly aids or abets the preparation or commission of a serious or an ordinary offence'), he immediately loses his temper.

As during the first meeting and in front of a such

an uninviting welcome, he fidgets, grows heated, rattling his spurs (which indicates violent annoyance), shoots flames through his eyes and then, listening to his heart and his heart only, rushes at them, hell-for-leather, and jumps at the throat of the most zealous of them. (Which today would be the equivalent of attacking a cop car.)

After which, he hurls insults at these *argousins*, as follows: *Ah! Infamous breed, too vile and grovelling for heaven to make known to you the virtue that lies in knight-errantry... Come now, band, not of archers, but of thieves, highway robbers...* (Which would be qualified today as contempt of a public official and law enforcement.)

It appears clearly, in reading this episode, that not only does Quixote never claim to be a follower of the prevailing authorities in order to legitimise his actions, but that he can slay them without any qualms if he considers them unfair, unwelcome or horribly barbaric.

This is what I am trying to express, perhaps in a reductive way, by declaring him an anarchist.

Having, in any case, nothing to lose, no position to protect at all costs, no comforting shelter in which to stagnate in peace.

Living on little.

Concerned about others.

Engaged in a merciless struggle against the bastards of every description.

Without gripping the handrail, without any kind of caution, or precaution, without any certainty of conquering, without retribution, without any mental reservations and without anyone's approval.

Driven by inner necessity and that savage energy, that fury, that fire which is one of the most significant traits of his person. A fire which draws its strength from the dream of knight-errantry that permeates his being, and has ripened in its depths, is rooted there and has slowly changed, like a seed in the earth, and made him a man whose love of freedom and sense of justice are written in his flesh, in his bones, down to the marrow.

The most remarkable thing about him, the most exceptional, it is that, in this will that clamours to change the course of things when they seem to him to be going the wrong way, the will to accomplish something big, beautiful, unforgettable, without ever backing out, he expects no gratitude, no medals, no flattery, no applause. He seeks no promotions, distinctions, or acknowledgement; he expects no advantage, no 'return on investments', as we moderns say.

Quixote is fundamentally sincere and fundamentally disinterested.

Ethically irreproachable, or almost. It's annoying.

The only problem is that more often than not, he has to pay the price.

5

For Quixote is not infallible. You ponderously insist on this point, sir, as if it gave you a malign pleasure to do so.

While it is true that Quixote puts his neck on the line, goes out on a limb, slogs it out with a rare boldness and valiance (is there any other way, sir, to get change happening?), he suffers the reality of battle in every bone of his body. In other words, more often than not, he gets it in the neck, unlike those soldiers with cushy postings who spout subversive rhetoric and feel themselves exempt from lifting a finger – a finger, which, by the way, is resting on a glass of Charmes-Chambertin which they sip, eyes half-closed in contentment, preferably in front of a roaring fire.

Every day, Quixote comes up against new enemies and the most formidable obstacles. You'd almost think that they intrigue him, that he yearns for them and looks forward with relish to fighting them. Could he be a sucker for punishment, bound and determined to wreck his life? Or does he rejoice at the perils in his path because they give him a chance to reveal hidden powers and surpass himself?

Every day he stumbles, trips over his feet just as he is getting a leg up, falls flat on his face, gets shot down in flames, and that is when he isn't beaten black and blue like the last of the losers, and returns from his forays much more the worse for wear than when he set out.

How are we to understand these failures?

Does Quixote provoke them to spare himself the shame of victory? For who is winning here, sir, if it is not the swindlers and the cheats?

Is he trying to expiate a crime? That of being alive, too alive?

Or does he seek to immolate himself, exalt in that Christian love of pain which led my beloved Pascal to wind a belt of nails around his waist?

What obscure reasons compel him to take such a bashing, over and over again? Where do they originate?

His recurrent failures never cease to intrigue me, sir, but I would never deign to explain your book to you. Still I would like to try going back in the chain of causes and effects, more thoroughly than you have done, to see what has led Quixote to so much defeat.

You, sir, know better than anyone for having been the object of ignoble usurpation, that all passionate readers – of which I am immeasurably one – endeavour to strip a book of its authorship. The reader squats the work, inhabits it, takes possession of it, remodels and diverts it to his or her very personal ends. In a word, the reader exploits it.

Which is what I am doing here, without the slightest trace of a scruple.

So, from my point of view, one of the most flagrant causes of Quixote's defeat is that he cannot, or will not, evaluate the balance of power. He cannot, or will not comprehend that resources, their plenitude or scarcity, are the sinews of war; that even the noblest cause cannot be won if it is not backed by a people, a party, an army, a brotherhood, devotees or a troop of fanatical affiliates.

As for Quixote, he wants the ends without possessing the means. But here's the situation: on the one hand we have a frail, isolated knight in makeshift armour who never gives a thought to how many enemies he has, a total novice in the strategies of war; and on the other hand, an unknown reality fraught with obstacles, some of which are terrifying.

To tackle this reality is as ill-advised as trying to halt an earthquake with pious words, or hope for peace on earth while knowing this depends on human beings. Sheer illusion!

Fair enough.

As a small group of Jews, foreigners and Communists who, though they hated war, formed the first resistants' groups in the 1940s, and with no hesitation threw themselves into a battle that was almost universally judged as doomed from the start; and as a young Chinese man, during the demonstrations of 1989 in Tiananmen Square, stood alone before a column of tanks to prevent them from advancing, so Quixote opposes powers hugely disproportionate to his own.

And it is because these powers are so unequal that the actions he undertakes with such fury, and wishes to be fearsome, end up down the plughole half the time. (Nabokov, who did a precise inventory of Quixote's victories and defeats, counted twenty victories, some of which are only partial, versus twenty defeats, which, all told, is not so bad.)

So if he fails twenty times in a row, it is because his initial ambition is titanic, and his battle colossal – nothing less than taking on the whole universe, as it will be written on his grave; nothing less than fighting the enslavement of the weakest, the injustice of the fittest and immunity of the filthy rotten bastards. But how does one hold back such a mighty river with nothing but one's hands?

If he fails, it is because a battle so ambitious, so immense, cannot be won alone. And Quixote is alone, alone, alone, in the most absolute and irremediable solitude.

With whom could he share this yearning for the highest peaks which burns within him?

Who but he would have the courage to pursue a dream which nothing guarantees will ever be fulfilled?

Who would put his future at stake to defend an idea of human dignity?

In that case, might solitude be the hero's condition, as it is the poet's?

Everything this morning leads me to think so.

Quixote is alone in thinking what he thinks and feeling what he feels; he is spontaneously averse to groups – I was going to say averse to packs – which generally mistreat him or make him an object of ridicule (behaviour which has the noteworthy tendency of strengthening the bonds within the pack).

But though solitude may be the price he pays for the singularity of his actions, it is also a deep-seated inclination which drives him into uninhabited mountains and melancholy forests with only birds for company, the murmurs of the trees and his faithful squire Sancho, far, far away from the tumult of the court, where powdered gentlemen, steeped in arrogance and skilled in the art of brown-nosing, strut like peacocks and do *ronds de jambe* until they drop.

Quixote will not breathe the same air as these people. That is his luxury.

He belongs to no pack and is alone in his battle. That is his weakness.

For the battle must be shored up by a wave of anger and a thousand beating hearts to have any chance of succeeding. All of History teaches us that, dear sir.

If he fails, it is because in such a battle, his weapons, which he puts at the service of justice, cannot vanquish on the basis of their power alone. Though force must sometimes be applied to ensure that the law is respected in the face of blind violence, force cannot, in the name of that law, wage murderous attacks, coerce refractory souls, and impose, with blows of the sword, the quixotic best of all possible worlds, without committing a worse injustice.

If he fails, it is because he misconstrues certain situations. Frequently he finds himself stuck in contexts quite comparable with ours when History, after a shock, becomes unreadable; when faced with its unpredictability, accelerations, storms and abrupt reversals, its enigmatic COVID-19s, we cannot pin it down to any intelligible pattern.

If he fails, it is because, in his megalomania, he aspires to resolve the philosophical question of evil, which since the dawn of Time has remained a yawning chasm, the black hole of Ethics.

But though he (obviously) does not resolve it, he has the great merit of bringing to light the maleficence camouflaged beneath the crust of pretending, unctuous urbanities, the discreet charm of a duke and duchess inwardly driven by the most sordid sentiments.

But to make this maleficence visible, to call it by its name, is an unpardonable fault in the eyes of those who want to doze in peace – much more unforgivable, moreover, than evil itself. Which explains the repeated thrashings inflicted upon our intrepid Quixote.

If he fails, it is because such a fight can never end, because such a fight can never be appeased, because the efforts it requires are constantly renewed, since nothing gained by man lasts forever, least of all freedom, and least of all justice.

Whence comes the feeling that, from one chapter to another, the same stories are endlessly linked and repeated *ad nauseam*, giving rise to what some, through sheer mental reflex have baptised 'running gags', the humour of repetition, which, when it doesn't bore me, sir – suffer me to tell you so – merely makes me sad.

This fight is endless, as I was saying, and so is the belief among men that somewhere lies a country where life is painless, a radiant, delightful country where the police are on holiday, the judges bored, the bastards idle, and writers talk about their work with humility – a country free of despots or any human filth, a merciful country, impossible to locate, always lacking, always long since lost; yet tirelessly we continue to await it.

This fight is endless, as is the inexpiable struggle against our human condition, its limitations, its fevers and its ordeals, its desperate precariousness, its nonsense in this godless world we have made for ourselves – I don't imagine you can conceive of such an aberration, sir – and against intractable death, which delimits it and always ends up planting her flag there, the bitch.

All these reasons, sir, which I have the indecency to inflict upon you in order to explain Quixote's repeated cock-ups, may be ill-founded. But my sad observation remains: your hidalgo often, very often, too often fails, which seems to me as unfair as it is undeserved; and far from being cause for amusement, it dismays me.

Especially since it suddenly occurs to me that Quixote fails, as today we may be failing to protect the planet. Because our planet is suffering, sir, our planet has a fever. Because our planet is suffocating and, if we do nothing, is in danger of going from bad to worse. Because we have bled it dry, sir, we have torn it up, exhausted, pillaged it, irremediably, perhaps. We have dishonoured it, sir, as your Quixote would say. My fear is that soon it will take on the colour of ashes.

Quixote dreamed of a fabulous life, a life modelled on that of the invincible knights described in the novels of Feliciano de Silva or Garci Rodriguez de Montalvo. But the books of the latter, which had enjoyed considerable success a few years earlier, are now disparaged. Too pretty, too manicured, too far from reality, the genre slowly expired.

You, my dear sir, are going to finish it off.

It is because under the reign of your King Felipe II, minds were growing disenchanted, the heyday of the epic was only a memory, the taste for the supernatural had slowly faded, and the romances of chivalry with their enchanting fairies, their four-tailed monsters and princesses locked up in unattainable towers who were delivered in extremis by rock-climbing champions who, with a single blow, split a treacherous knight in two, these novels were increasingly seen as dangerously anachronistic, deleterious to serious minds. The latter invited us to look directly at reality in its rawest form; to respect the prevailing institutions, in particular that of marriage; and to reasonably stick to a few safe values in order to maintain an economy which, after the euphoria linked to the discovery of America, was starting to run into its first difficulties. Dreams and utopias, advocated by the big-hearted heroes of chivalric novels, are in no way values one can bank on with certainty. Much better that they be banned.

Quixote learns this the hard way.

He hoped to drive back injustice in lieu of reining back the sea. He suffers indignities in return.

He wanted to triumph and lay down his laurels at the feet of Dulcinea. He falls into the mud and narrowly escapes disaster.

He wanted solemnity, the airs of an emperor, eternal glory, in capital letters. He ends up flat on his face, bleeding, with four shattered teeth.

He hoped to experience an extraordinary epic and to make his life the most beautiful of masterpieces. His adventure is a farce – stuffing – and he is the turkey.

He wanted to reconcile his dream with reality. His dream was smashed to pieces on the reefs of reality. And reality brutally triumphs, intractable reality, prosaic reality, obscene reality that is ready to dispense every kind of cruelty and devastation – and always has the final word.

He who wanted to be sublime, and hoped to flit from triumph to triumph by dint of desire and stubbornness, is treated like a beggar and a clown, chased off with stones, as was Paul Cézanne, in his time, when he went to the Jas studio, pursued by sneaky children who bombarded him with pebbles, with the tacit permission of their parents from Aix, who considered the painter a failure. This memory just came into my mind and makes me sad, as always.

He who hoped to pit himself against the giants of the earth and make them eat dust, as Amadis of Gaul did before him, or his brother Galaor, less of a crybaby; he who expected to climb to the highest peaks to the sound of bugles of victory, now hears only the jeering laughter and sneering sarcasm of those who are only too glad to see him defeated.

He who aspired to the highest heights falls to the deepest depths, tumbles like reckless Icarus who, like him, overestimated his strength.

The drunkenness of combat dissipated (drunkenness is the word, because there is something about Don Quixote that resembles an exultation, a high, a secret thrill in fighting and striking out), so here he is on the ground 'with an obligation to pursue, and rough reality to embrace' (this quote, which no student of the upper six today would dare slip into an essay, so often has it been used since 1871, will speak to you, it seems to me).

He then realises that between the world of his dreams and the one he bumps up against, day after day, there is an abyss; between what he had madly desired and the wormy fruits he irritably picks; between the fabulous horseback rides of the 'Knight of Sad Countenance', protected by his good fairy Urgande, and his harebrained experiences on the pebbly roads of La Mancha, with not the slightest potion to drink nor even the shadow of a fairy on the horizon.

His error, his unpardonable error, was to take literature literally, take its fictions for cash.

Literature lied to him. Literature ripped him off. Literature dangled before his nose a world that did not exist. Literature is nothing but a web of lies and mystifications.

Literature is a scam.

And those who create it are crooks (some of whom, one must admit, are not lacking in charm).

All illusions spent, Quixote loses his footing. He wobbles. His certainties are crumbling. His anger fades away – a bad sign. His grandiose plans are denied one after the other.

Would the world be that vale of tears, whose existence Sancho reminds him of, just in time?

As if he were emerging from a dream, an anxious lucidity suddenly returns to him: he has fought in vain.

I was born, he confides to Sancho, *to live while dying*.

Melancholy words.

Everything is falling apart. He is no longer the torchbearer of knight-errantry; of chivalry. Nor is he the equal of the sublime Amadis, or the saviour of the weak and destitute, or the implacable rectifier of wrongs caused by human baseness.

Now that he has come back to earth, he is no longer swashbuckling in the least, and no longer prides himself on being of godly origin.

He is just a man like any other. A bruised, unhappy, miserable man reduced, as the result of a defeat, to his flaws, cracks and failings.

I, sir, do not take myself for Neptune, nor do I try to make anyone take me for an astute man, for that I am not. I would simply like to convince the world of the error it makes in not reviving in itself the happy times of knight-errantry.

Sad and disenchanted, he rediscovers the ancient disharmony, the poison of failure, the gratuitousness of evil, and the immortal amorality of men: their hatred, their cunning, their ingratitude, their passion to destroy and their appetite for betrayal.

All the bitter knowledge.

Reality regained.

And this reality has a foul taste, and this reality is ugly, and this reality is of unspeakable ferocity, and the nightmares there are real, and life there is inhuman.

He rediscovers the misery of his crippled body, the harsh rusticity of inns, the infinite fatigue of travel, and his own powerlessness, which he is forced to acknowledge.

He becomes disillusioned.

His castles in Spain are collapsing.

And his belief that men could be better and that he could help to make them better dissipates for a moment.

I did say a moment.

Because if you believe he is resigned, you don't know Quixote very well.

Anyone, in his position, would have laid down his arms. Not he!

Quixote is made of tougher leather.

Indestructible.

Or made of the stuff of a hero whom adversity, far from making him discouraged, straightens and strengthens him.

Quixote retains, come wind and high water, a despotic desire for justice and life that nothing alters and nothing destroys.

Men do have some flaws, he says, but it is always possible to defeat them.

How? asks Sancho naively.

Through generosity and greatness of soul, the only attitudes worth anything in the face of human imperfection and wickedness, which is another name for misfortune, he replies, in essence (unless I've invented these words, as I have sometimes surprised myself doing).

It is the only answer for those who do not want to be inferior to their dreams and in spite of turmoil, try to remain the best they can be.

And what is remarkable is that, despite the setbacks, despite the hailstones of invective, the stinging disappointments, snubs, affronts and outrages, the blows received that give him this 'rueful countenance', the suppressed distress that current opinion ascribes to the *poètes maudits*, the mute desolation engraved on his face and in the depths of his eyes, Quixote endures his trials by disdaining to complain.

No bitterness, never a sigh, a sob, or a regret. Never the slightest lament.

Never deceit either, nor the desire to punish others, and even less to injure, dominate or enslave them.

Never a cunning project of revenge, the slightest resentment or ulterior motive.

Only the conduct of a hidalgo of exemplary dignity.

Quixote is ethically (almost) perfect. It's annoying.

6

And since you make your Quixote a loser, allow me to tell you, sir, that he is a beautiful loser. For if he fails in relation to the goal he has given himself, he succeeds, always and everywhere he goes, in creating life around him.

Wherever he goes, sir, a great wind starts to blow.

Wherever he goes, wherever he is unleashed, I should say, everywhere where sleep threatens to triumph, he shakes things up, asks questions, disturbs and astonishes, he overturns foregone conclusions, disrupts the usual points of reference, loosens tongues, mobilises affects, destabilises routines, provokes yearning, lets in rushes of new air, and creates what Guy Debord, a thinker dear to my generation, called 'situations'.

No more endless boredom.

Habits expire.

Consciousness is raised.

Desires break loose and run free, as people said in 1968.

A sort of emulation spreads. The air grows sharp. Laughter erupts, and cruelties ensue.

Whether he enters an inn or the middle of a field, his presence immediately disrupts the dull monotony of things, sometimes quite in spite of himself.

New arrangements are created between protagonists, new forces emerge.

And life bursts forth, indispensable, churning, unpredictable life, contradictory, dark, tremulous and full of promise.

Wherever he goes, he spreads fire, fever and turbulence which force us to think.

Wherever he goes, he awakens minds wallowing in their dew-ponds, sparks debate, blows on embers, kindles dormant passion in some and in others awakens the pleasure of the new, the daring, and the dangerous. In a word: Adventure.

Master of turmoil, he transports into the heart of the hurricane people, beasts, and everything which, before he arrived, were plodding along in soporific boredom.

And in the same way that he upsets spatial, social and emotional order, this troublemaker upsets temporal order, too.

Because time for him is not that linear, flat and horribly monotonous, stingy, measured and measurable time that is imposed on human beings, who must at all costs make their labour pay.

For this man, unexposed to sacrosanct social work and its sacrosanct servitudes, time is of another kind, because it is determined by himself, determined by his passion. And this time of which he is master is supple, lively, whimsical, released from chronology, a time capable of linking today and yesterday, and which now is impossible to remotely imagine.

Which explains why any reference to the past he makes is not, contrary to what we might at first think, the product of a rancid attachment to the past, nostalgic clinging to worm-eaten ideas, values full of moth-holes like the clothes on his back. His references to the happy times of knight-errantry are simply the product of another concept of time, one which Quixote perceives in the way that summer can suddenly arrive in winter, childhood blossom in adulthood, an old enterprise suddenly appear very *au courant*, and a step backward in the face of stupidity constitute a most interesting development.

In your time, was this conception already incongruous, as one would tend to think now, in this world where we live walled up between a phantom past and a future full of fear; in this world, so to speak without the passage of time, in this world of an everlasting present? (Which, by the way, leads some writers, in order to be up-to-date, never to use old grammatical rags like the *passé simple*, and politicians not to give a damn about the ozone layer when it has no effect on their immediate power, and even less about the fate of 'fellow humans who will survive them'.)

Quixote turns everything upside down.

He's the Fire Maker.

The instigator of permanent insurrection whose other name is Life.

A real wave-making machine.

However, his main intention is not to shock or to provoke in vain. He is not driven by an obsession with racket. He is no chic extremist, comfortably ensconced in the excess that is the stock in trade of his small-scale business.

Disorder for disorder's sake is by no means his aim (although he is fond of stirring it up, sometimes, in passing, to impress the ladies and damsels).

He simply wishes to restore the order of knights errant and to combat realities he finds unacceptable, which he believes it is his job to remedy. Which inevitably leads him to resist the established order. And sometimes (one has to acknowledge) turn this order upside down.

But as you know, sir, acts of resistance bring upheaval and scandal. It was true yesterday, and it is true today. There's no point in denying it, and may the high-minded forgive me.

Quixote, Christlike? Some have claimed that he is. It is true that he does not bring peace but the sword, which radically marks the divide between the just and the unjust and as a result, breaks down the prevailing dynamics in the society of his time.

I could go quite far in comparing Quixote with the figure of Christ and endeavour to highlight their points in common.

But I will limit myself for the moment to remarking that Quixote is allergic to half-heartedness; he always takes the defence of the weak, constantly evokes an ideal realm that does seem out of this world; goes riding on his swayback nag to a fictional Jerusalem; flies into terrible rages, well worth those described by Matthew (21:12-13); shows himself to be infinitely good under his rough exterior; grants ladies of pleasure the same courteous attention he does ladies in jewels and lace (but none comes to wipe his feet with her long hair); he does not give a damn about titles, ranks, grades, levels and other labels; he never lets himself enter into temptation (although…); everywhere he goes, he stirs up a wind of Sacred Madness that conveys values that cannot be found on any stock exchange; and like the Other he suffers a thousand and one torments, so that like the Other he never ceases to die and resurrect.

Christlike or not, Quixote can only gravely disrupt the tidy order that prevails.

Especially since, in a Spain immobilised by the standards laid down by the Crown in addition to the power of the Catholic Church, the slightest gesture that deviates from these standards immediately appears to be a terrible threat.

Suspicion runs rampant, with no limits.

It verges on insanity.

The first statute of purity of blood was promulgated against the Jews in 1449.

As for the Inquisition, established in 1478, it wreaked terror again and again throughout the territory. A careless word, a religious expletive thoughtlessly uttered, an accusation of lust, adultery or another of these abominable devilries, a denunciation on the grounds of being an atheist or a practitioner of witchcraft (the exercise of denunciation is not only a sport of the French), and you are flung alive into the flames, beheaded, imprisoned, excommunicated or banished.

And this terror grew even more under Inquisitor General Archbishop of Seville, who in 1559 organised one of the most impressive autos-da-fé in all of history.

The same year, the first Spanish Index of Forbidden Books was published and included those of Feliciano de Silva. Book hell was filled to the brim.

And certificates of blood purity, *limpiezas de sangre*, were starting to be distributed to the 'unsullied' of Jewish or Muslim blood.

Felipe II, King of the Spains and its Dependencies in the Mediterranean and the Americas, who acceded to the throne in 1555, only prolonged this infamous policy and kept the country living under a pall of fear, a country in which nothing must cause the slightest disorder, either in people's minds or social organisation.

To be in motion, to be alive, speak, laugh, breathe, fight, it is necessary to shake up this perfect, motionless order which can be summed up as follows:

- the poor: in their poverty (which no one contests);

- courtiers (and all their precious species): in their barnyard;

- deviants: at the stake;

- harmful books: reduced to ashes.

The fact of being on the move is necessarily worrying to those who have bled life of its pulse, passion and thunder and who live petrified and tormented, trembling with the slightest breath they take, trying to be forgotten and at the same time forgetting to live, mired in apathy, in torpor, and that is not to say a kind of death, which they call peace.

In the eyes of the latter, disturbances are only tolerable if they are justified, deemed legal and moral by power: the power of the Church and the power of the king, during your era, the power of money today, which has replaced the two others at a profit.

Basically, sir, things have not changed. Except in name.

7

I said in a previous letter, sir, that your Quixote was an anarchist to the core. And, with all due respect, I maintain that it is true.

Because this man, though fragile in appearance, possesses a power of affirmation, a power of severance, refusal in the face of things that are supposed to be self-evident. This power, in short, is political, in the noblest sense of the word, a kind encountered only rarely. Your Quixote, sir, is an anarchist to the core. Bakunin himself could not have given that speech Quixote delivered to the goatherds.

In summary he says: What happy times and what a happy age were those when people didn't know the words 'yours' and 'mine', and all things were commonly owned (no more private property), and Justice was not impeded by the favour and self-interest which now squeeze the life from it (no more class justice), and young women needed not fear neither brazen tongues nor criminal intent (#MeToo, four centuries ahead of its time).

All this has been lost and defiled in this calamitous century, he adds.

But to remedy the situation, knight-errantry

was instituted, and he is its torchbearer – he to whom *heaven has given birth in this age of iron,* and whose vocation is *to revive what is referred to as the golden age.* Specifically, to restore justice in the face of the defenceless, to sway ill-intentioned hearts, settle quarrels, wash away insults, defend abused young girls, protect widows, foster orphans, assist the destitute and helpless, and fight a ruthless battle against felons, the wicked, scoundrels, and all those who abuse their power in one way or another: all that, and nothing less!

In other words, he wishes to bring about a more just, lofty and melodious humanity, a world where no one will force anyone to kneel anymore, a humanity in which new ways of living will be invented; and to create ties without despotic powers poking their noses everywhere.

For Quixote distrusts power, all kinds of power. And he does not hesitate to attack the most unassailable and terrifying institutions in the kingdom – I'm mainly thinking of the *Santa Hermandad.*

The *Santa Hermandad*, created by Isabella the Catholic in 1476, had made the Spanish people quake for a century because it combined two equally coercive powers: the power of the Crown and the power of the Church.

The institution was composed of groups of armed men whose holy mission was to track down and apprehend criminals of all kinds.

These militias formed a centralised and efficient police force, endowed with far-reaching powers of jurisdiction. In a sense, it was the ancestor of the militias which flourished during the Second World War and are still rampant in many countries today.

These militias are formed on the model of the old *Hermandades* – brotherhoods. Fraternal militias! I bid you to savour the perversion, the ugliness contained in the juxtaposition of these two words, which, better than any speech, express the violence and boorishness (anointed with Holy Oils) that drive these formidable police forces.

(Remember that, originally, the old *Hermandades*, the brotherhoods which these new militias claim to belong to, but of which they are only dreadful distortions, had a completely different, if not totally opposite, vocation: they were made up of peasants in revolt against the injustice of the nobles and their abuse of power; they were peasants who did not shy away from fomenting insurrections and attacking fortresses and castles – end of parenthesis.)

Quixote will act so assertively and so effectively against this *Santa Hermandad* (see the episode of the galley slaves) that it will issue a warrant for his arrest.

But the *Santa Hermandad* is not the only institution that Quixote, through his actions, singles out and challenges. He seems to be very suspicious of the religious institution, which, moreover, he in no way confuses with the saints who made his glory: Saint George, Saint Martin, Saint Paul or Saint James the Moor-slayer, whom he deeply admires and to whom he does not hesitate to compare himself (we know his penchant for braggadocio): *For these saints and knights were of the same profession as myself, which is the calling of arms. They were saints, and fought with divine weapons, and I am a sinner and fight with human ones.*

As I was saying, Quixote is highly suspicious of the religious institution, its fanatic violence which Voltaire later qualified as despicable, the blind submission it demands of all, and its appetite for suffering that is supposed to redeem sinful souls but which somewhat taints the joys and ecstasies promised by Jesus. None of which he ever clearly states, of course, due to the prevailing censorship, but which his actions betray in the most obvious ways, as in the following episode – allow me, dear sir, to remind you of the details: one day Quixote meets a little convoy that one could not imagine more peaceable in appearance. But at the mere sight of two Benedictine monks escorting a carriage (which contained a lady from Biscay) surrounded by men on horseback and two servants on foot, he flies into a rage.

What is eating him? No one knows. The fact is that Quixote, prone to bouts of fever which lead him to imagine the worst, without the slightest grounds accuses the two poor monks of kidnapping a princess. He calls them vile perjurers, diabolical scoundrels and other very derogatory names (which usually serve as safety valves for the surplus of rage that inhabits him in angry moods but perhaps above all, the surplus of sadness he has accumulated inside). Unable to contain himself, he digs his heels into the sides of his Pegasus and flies at them.

His implicit reticence, his wild hostility towards the religious body is so obvious that it leads Sancho (who prides himself on the *limpieza* of his blood, and tirelessly repeats, as he has been trained to do, that he is a fervent Catholic and that he knows his *Pater Noster* by heart, two precautions are better than one), that it leads Sancho, as I was saying, to recklessly declare, in speaking of his master, that *he could not be more secular*. He omits, moreover, to adopt the scandalised tone that is *de rigueur* when one is making such statements (which, at the time, were downright revolting).

More serious still is that Quixote savagely attacks the hooded penitents who walk in a procession, brandishing the icon of the Virgin Mary, although they have caused him no harm.

Lashing out at the Immaculate Conception! At the Impeccable (literally: without sin, in Latin *impeccabilis*, from *im-*'not' and *peccare* 'to sin')! Lashing out at the purer than Pure! The mother of *Iesum Christum qui resurrexit a mortuis, ascended ad caelos, sedet ad dexteram Dei Patris omnipotentis!*

Horror and damnation! O crime of crimes! Sacrilege of sacrileges!

Quixote has overstepped the most divinely sacred limits of religion.

I shit on the Christian name, wrote Artaud in the twentieth century, and these words greatly shocked the bourgeois.

One can easily imagine the effect of Don Quixote's attack on a holy procession under the reign of the Very Catholic Felipe II (because that is what he was called), a king whose piety is as enthusiastic as his taste for sex and his hatred of his son (whom he will have arrested and very probably murdered), and whose motto is quite simply: *Dominus mihi adjutor* – God is my assistant (on a permanent contract basis, with benefits, I hope).

With Quixote's brutal onslaught, the unthinkable suddenly heaves into view. Absolute transgression. Unforgivable infamy. The most appalling sin imaginable in a Christian land.

Now, sir, you are not unaware that the fiercer the censorship, the more numerous the prohibitions, the stricter the police forces and the more coercive the laws, the more intense the cravings for that which is forbidden and the dark forces of seduction that blasphemy awakens.

This, most certainly, is one of the keys to your book's immense success.

Of course, you take the precaution of explaining that there had been a misunderstanding on the part of Quixote, that though it sounds crazy, he simply did not recognise the Holy Virgin and acted recklessly, out of sheer thoughtlessness, and is in no way the dangerous iconoclast that appearances might at first suggest. Never mind! The thing is written black on white, and secretly enchants the Spaniards, who live muzzled under the iron rule of the Church.

This transgression avenges them.

In fact, Quixote's major grievance against the religious institution (without ever stating it openly, I repeat) is obviously the wild censorship that it exerts upon his books.

Everyone still remembers how in 1500, Cardinal Cisneros, Archbishop of Toledo, ordered the destruction, in a gigantic auto-da-fé, of more than a million works, and that in 1559 the Inquisitor General and Archbishop of Seville organised an even more fearsome auto-da-fé.

As if that were not enough, the Catholic monarchs promulgated a decree prohibiting printers and booksellers from printing books without their permission.

And in 1559, the *First Redemptive Index of Forbidden Books* was published at the expense of the Inquisition.

So, sir, you have reason to worry about the ferocious censorship perpetrated by the religious authorities and the Crown.

And one can easily understand that in your novel you entrusted a priest (assisted by a barber) with the care of expurgating from Don Quixote's library the chivalric romances presumed guilty for his presumed madness, with the exception of a few rarities like the famous *Amadís de Gaula* by Feliciano de Silva and the no-less-famous *Tirant lo Blanc: a Treasure of Good Humour and a Mine of Entertainment.*

As for the book *La Galatea* by a certain Miguel de Cervantes, it does not lack a certain inventiveness, as you mischievously say to the expurgating monk, who added 'but we will have to wait until the publication of the second part to make a serious judgement as to its literary merits.'

In the meantime, a proposal is made to solidly wall up the door of the library in order to avoid any spread of the virus.

But back to the question of power. Sancho too shares his master's instinctive distrust.

When during a cruel parody (the reading of which not only did not amuse me for a second, but darkened my spirits for a whole day), organised by a duke and a duchess always ready to amuse themselves at the expense of the weakest and most helpless, when Sancho is made to believe that he has been made governor of the archipelago of Barataria, at first he can no longer contain himself and swells with pride.

He begins by establishing a centre-right regime: aid to peasants, the maintenance of privileges for nobles, clearing out idlers, thieves, beggars and vagabonds with a Kärcher pressure washer, and absolute respect for religion and Churchmen; carries out his political duties with great wisdom (like

Henry the Impotent, Charles VI, Joanna the Mad, Ludwig II of Bavaria or the depressive Paul Deschanel, to name only a few); keeps his head in all circumstances; does not succumb to the vertigo of power that (almost) infallibly strikes those who govern us. Better: quite soon, he finds himself hating this function that he had so eagerly coveted. And after seven days of reigning in the vast ducal palace, he is overcome by a rising tide of sadness and loneliness.

He then realises that having succumbed to ambition has only brought him anxiety and torment.

Don Quixote had warned him: *Public offices are like a sea strewn with reefs.*

On this occasion he had whispered several pieces of advice on how to best manage his government (the exact opposite advice of that which was generously provided, one century before your time, by Niccolò Machiavelli, who believed that first, the Prince had to learn how not to be good, and secondly, he had to free himself without any qualms from the ideals of Justice and the Good if he wanted to be somewhat operational).

In short, Quixote had proposed to Sancho a sort of Charter, which all men of power would do well to use as their inspiration and which is partially transcribed as follows:

You must examine yourself and try to know yourself, which is the most difficult knowledge that one can imagine. This will prevent you from getting puffed up like the frog who wanted to make himself as big as an ox; and the very thought that you were once the pig-herd in your village will prevent you from fanning out your tail, like the peacock of the fable when he sees the ugliness of his feet.

Do not let yourself be guided by arbitrary laws, so much favoured by the ignorant who take themselves for great minds.

May the tears of the poor incline you to more compassion – but not to more justice – than the pleadings of the rich.

Strive to discover the truth through the promises and presents of the rich, as through the tears and the entreaties of the poor.

Whenever fairness permits, do not overwhelm the offender with the full extent of the law, for the reputation of a stern judge does not stand higher than that of the compassionate one.

If you bend the rod of justice, let it be under the weight of mercy and not under that of gifts.

If you happen to have to judge one of your enemies, forget that he offended you and only consider the facts.

Don't indulge your personal passions when you judge the cause of another, for the errors you will thereby commit will most frequently be irremediable.

If a pretty woman comes to ask you for justice, turn away your eyes from her tears and your ears from her sighs; consider her request calmly, if you don't want her to sweep away your reason.

To this list, Quixote had added, not without an inner smile, some subsidiary advice that may prove to be politically decisive such as:

- do not belch in public;
- do not fart, even mentally (I permit myself to add this);
- drink temperately and dine sparingly, scrupulously avoiding garlic and onion: condiment preferred by boors (and heartbreaking frustration for Sancho);
- take care of your garments by putting on a doublet, the latest style of cape and full breeches, instead of these shapeless short ones that hide the arse;
- avoid piling up and stringing together proverbs at random;
- ride a horse with distinction and not sagging like a flan;
- and never, ever quibble about the nobility of a lineage, because about such matters, the Iberians are touchy to an almost pathological degree.

But despite these valuable recommendations, Sancho, weary of not being able to eat as he pleases, weary of listening to supplicants who cover him with anathema when they do not win their case, weary of having to act as a warlord, he who flees from the slightest skirmish and does not share the warlike inclinations of his master, weary and more than weary of power and its servitude, for which he has no inclination or craving, because when it comes to governing, I do not understand it any better than a vulture, Sancho chooses to blow off his title of governor and regain his lost freedom, in other words to:

- sleep in the shade of an oak and not in silky Dutch sheets;

- live with his head in the clouds, taking it easy, rather than breaking his behind on an angular throne;

- lunch on the fresh grass rather than on silver dishes;

- lunch on a crust of black bread rather than a roast pigeon with olives, of which he is very fond;

- walk in rope sandals rather than with cramped feet in Cordoba leather;

- and return to his beloved master, rather than suffer the horrible obligations to which the powerful are permanently subjected, surrounded by scoundrels devoid of backbone and repugnantly obsequious.

Sancho, it is decided, will remain poor and the sole governor… of his goats!

A magnificent lesson in freedom, soberly greeted by Quixote in the following terms:

Freedom is one of the most precious gifts that heaven has bestowed upon men.

Quixote, sir, is an anarchist, I maintain and repeat. His whole existence attests to this.

Money? The least we can say is that Quixote is troubled with severe contradictions about it. In other words, he has nothing, truly nothing in common with the raptors nowadays called businessmen.

To the ecclesiastic who, in chapter XXXII, orders him to return home to manage his property and stop his vain and ridiculous vagrancy, he answers, quivering with rage:

Some take the broad road of overweening ambition; others that of mean and servile flattery; others that of deceitful hypocrisy, and some that of true religion; but I, led by my star, follow the narrow path of knight-errantry, and in pursuit of that calling I despise wealth, but not honour.

Don Quixote despises money but not honour. The universal mania of hoarding, hoarding and more hoarding does not touch him for a single moment.

The project of making a fortune, even a modest one, never crosses his mind.

His little personal interests never infringe upon his superior ideas.

He is not possessed by the pleasure of possessing. Moreover, it remains every bit as foreign to him as erotic pleasure.

In short, Quixote does not have a credit card in place of a heart, as my mother would have said, for her way of speaking was often full of imagery, like that of Sancho.

On the other hand, leaving an inn without paying is by no means a problem for him, for the excellent reason that the law of chivalry states that all knights-errant must be graciously accommodated in recompense for the good they spread all around them. Normal.

Opulence? He is totally indifferent to it, and lives, by choice, like the poorest of the poor.

But his poverty is spontaneously generous, the opposite of proprietary wealth, which is almost always spontaneously stingy. Having nothing to make money from, nothing to sell and nothing to take, Quixote gives his passion, his ardour and his vigour.

Moreover, far from being a painful deprivation or a degrading impoverishment, his destitution is an experience that inspires and strengthens him, delivers him from the pangs and servitude caused by possession.

His destitution is the very condition of his freedom.

Quixote is in no way tempted by these material objects of concupiscence which today, dear sir, have become for many a reason for living and for bumping off those who stand in the way of their massive appetite.

A convinced proponent of de-growth, he believes that good food, capon supremes, overpriced delicacies and the afternoon nap were created for gentlemen who bask in the courtyard.

He lives from day to day; he sometimes sleeps under the stars; he is content to sup on a piece of bread as black as his armour, accompanied not by a slice of ham but a piece of cheese so hard that he could break a giant's head with it. His aperitif: pure water from streams; his mattress: an austere heap of straw; and his water closet: wild nature and some chestnut leaves. What more could you want?

His temper? Often angry to the point of ferocity because he neither wants or knows how to deal with his time. Or negotiate with all that is implied therein of cunning, pressure, calculation, scheming and, sometimes, underhand manœuvres. Or compromise. Or connive. Or engage in clandestine wheeling and dealing, or swine hustling. Or make lily-livered, mediocre trade-offs with them.

Quixote could have as his motto, like Erasmus: *Concedo nulli* (I yield to nobody).

He loathes careful doses, skimping, quibbling and half-measures, both in his efforts to redeem the world and in the field (field!) of love.

In the land of Don Quixote, one does not skimp on these things…

He is just as unaware of this flaccid and now-fashionable virtue called resilience, a word whose continual misuse has completely bastardised its meaning. Resilience is sold cut-rate among the so-called adaptive strategies ('You were beaten up? Take it with a smile!' or 'Adopt the French spirit: be elegant even in misfortune!') in a package including the word 'to share', which the beautiful people take great pleasure in repeating, along with the words 'fraternity', 'human rights' and others of equally noble stature, all pronounced with the extreme gravity and dignity of the undisputed humanist, and when I hear them, inspire the most outrageous stupidities in me.

Quixote always arrives at just the wrong moment, he is inopportune. A hothead. Unruly.

Our stubborn habit of living is not enough for him.

Nothing interests him, in the end, but the sky that is impossible to embrace.

Impatient, dazzling, he does not advance but melts. He melts into the immense sky that he would like to seize and with a single gesture, bring down to earth, bring down upon this unattainable thing he tirelessly assails and which tirelessly evades him.

He is reckless; he prefers the shadow of hope to prey.

And he fights for a cause he finds remarkable – too bad if it fails, and too bad if it's hopeless, and too bad if it sometimes makes him suffer atrociously!

At least the beauty of his actions will remain, along with the satisfaction of having ardently defended them.

Should we prefer those in whom no fire burns?

Should we prefer the lukewarm and the apathetic, submissive as larvae, whose only concern is not to make waves?

Should we prefer the mute and the cowards who chastely close their eyes before everything that pisses them off?

'We moan, we are silent, we have supper, we forget.'

Or the two-faced, the scumbags and deserters, who cover their faces and make themselves scarce, as almost all of us do today, collectively and unflinchingly, before the miseries of the world, whether they go by the name of Kutupalong or Lampedusa.

8

This morning, dear sir, I am dying to ask you a question about Don Quixote's deep longing for freedom and justice, and his obvious hostility towards power. Would these attitudes by any chance be yours?

Excuse me for putting my foot in it, but it seems to me that your knight is quite a convenient scapegoat.

Indeed, I get the feeling that you have him endorse anything you cannot say openly; and that, skilfully, you make him give others a piece of your mind, to the effect that the end of the last century and the beginning of the new one are calamitous, to say the least; that the Catholic, Apostolic and Roman Church is evil as well as omnipotent, and the same goes for its police forces; that in both, laziness, idleness, gluttony and sluggishness triumph every day; that no gentlemen is worthy of his title, unlike you-know-who; and that they claim to serve the king while cleaning their nails – in other words it's no skin off their back.

You have him barrel straight into everything that is rotten or questionable in the kingdom of Spain, everything of which, I suppose, your conscience disapproves without your being able to say so, and which you have him reveal as innocently as you please.

You go so far as to make him embody the incredible dream of equality among men, an equality that is obviously not the one inscribed in our texts of law today but which has to do with harmony, balance, agreement.

For one can say of knight-errantry, as of love, that it makes all things equal, Quixote asserts, verbatim.

Indeed, Quixote, does not give a damn about titles, ratings, coteries and other social fictions, so foreign are these to his spirit of justice and deep kindness. For him, they are nothing but nonsense. And our knight-errant has other fish to fry!

All beings, in his eyes, are worthy of respect, whatever their legacy, their origin and their position in the social scale. Everyone, he says, is the son of his works, and what does lineage matter. For blood is an inheritance, but virtue an acquisition, and virtue is of one hundred times the value of blood (these are his own words).

The same goes for women.

When he tells Sancho that he is always ready to defend their honour, he makes a point of specifying: whoever they may be. Whether they are whores, peasants or princesses, he views them without prejudice. Moreover, he constantly confuses them with each other, and shows all – and I mean all – the most exquisite courtesy.

Your Quixote is such a stranger, I was saying, to social categories and impassable borders that separate beings, so innocent before these things and so candid that it never occurs to him to condescend to use the speech of the common man with the common man, even if it means not being understood by him. I think of Maritorne and the innkeeper's wife, who understand about as much of his language as if he were speaking Greek, which makes them quietly laugh and elbow each other. I think of the amazed labourers whom he addresses in verse embellished with the rarest epithets; and to the three peasant women (one of whom is supposed to be Dulcinea) who unceremoniously send him packing because they understand nothing of his words, which they have never heard before and will never hear again, just like the antics he performs as a worthy representative of the knight-errantry.

As for me, sir, it is the language of traders that I find impossible to listen to.

Would you like me to translate the word 'traders' for you? It designates people addicted to financial pornography. You don't know what financial pornography is? Carry on, dear sir. Carry on.

Quixote, as I was saying, speaks the same superb

language to everyone, and never uses it as a means of intimidating those who possess neither his vocabulary nor his culture.

He does not make a crowd-pleasing slogan of his desire for a better world. He does not trumpet it from the rooftops like the smug professional liars of politics who seek to win the title of high-minded souls, when all that motivates them is the desire to manipulate.

Have you noticed, sir, that the latter's fear of missing out on some late-breaking outrage sometimes leads them to poorly disguise their secret desire for power? Have you noticed that their secret desire for power, most of the time, is camouflaged as its opposite? Quixote is no more oratorical and poetic about his great sentiments and great love of humanity. He is probably 'not French enough for that'.

He does not claim to be seditious like our artists who specialise in subsidised subversion and our token rebels who parade across the sets of liberal television networks and affix their signature at the bottom of all the manifestos.

The values he defends, those that were revealed to him in chivalric romances and filed away in his heart are by no means frills with which to embroider his speeches. They in no way resemble the fancy rhetorical needlework so dear to our tribunes, or the powder thrown in the eyes of the gape-mouthed crowds who await the holy incantations of the big boss to rain down upon them. And if he applies them (his values), it is because he cannot do otherwise than to put them to use, without the detours of reflection and beyond all dogma. Beyond all authority. Drawn straight from their wellspring at the heart of life.

'By intuition': I don't know how to say it better than that.

Moved by reasons of the heart which reason knows nothing about, as Pascal would say.

In a non-ratoid manner, Musil would add.

In that Europe where rationalism will soon take hold of every mind, Quixote acts as if he were driven by an irrepressible necessity, an impulse as imperious as it is inexplicable, an unformulated intuition that is more sure and more lucid than any form of knowledge, a wild unknown thing, irreducible to any logical explanation, which boils in him like blood, and overflows.

It is in his bond with Sancho that the values for which he fights are embodied in the most obvious way, especially the value of equality.

Quixote thinks that Sancho, though a peasant, has the makings of a governor (oh that one day our National Assembly, which includes only a tiny number of men and women who practise a manual trade, may be inspired by him!), and does not have to kowtow to anyone, and even less to serve anyone or obey like a dog summoned with a whistle.

He does not expect Sancho to show that hypocritical deference obligatorily simulated by an inferior in the face of his lord and master, cap in hand, head lowered, eyes cast towards the ground.

On the contrary, he urges Sancho to be proud of his origins: *Draw glory, Sancho, your humble birth, and don't be ashamed to say that you are peasant-born; for when it is seen that you are not ashamed, no one will try to make you blush.*

In a word, he invites him to consider himself as being as one with him: *I want you to sit by my side, in the company of these good people, and that you be but one with me, who am your lord and master; that you eat from my dish and drink what I will drink.*

Sancho has understood him so well that he allows himself to affectionately tease Don Quixote, and burst into laughter – though without an ounce of malevolence – at each of his innumerable mistakes, or mischievously parody the heroic-sublime speeches that go to his master's head like wine, when, contradicted by facts, they fall flat.

At other times he bitterly complains about his master's extravagances, and utters scathing but justified reproaches (which Don Quixote takes without losing his calm), and refuses to feign a relationship of equality by replying tit for tat to his advances, saying he much prefers to eat alone, and in peace.

The question of equality, which in Antiquity was one of the foundations of Athenian democracy, will again be posited, violently, a few decades after you; and it is not the least of your merits, dear sir, to have given it a significant boost. This is how we recognise a genius. I wanted to save my compliments for later, but this is too good an occasion to miss by consigning myself to silence.

There is the proof, in the case that it were needed, sir, that all utopias are destined to come true one day or another. Whence comes the ferocious hostility directed at them by those people who want, at all costs, to keep things exactly as they are, no matter how abject; those people whom I believe to be (lousy, rotten) conservatives or reactionaries.

Your hidalgo, dear sir, is quite the opposite, both in his dreams and his actions.

No wonder that Spain, of all the countries in the world, and throughout its history, is the one which has seen the greatest growth and prosperity in the libertarian movement.

No wonder the CNT (National Confederation of Labour) founded in 1910 and the FAI (Iberian Anarchist Federation), founded in 1927, have had more power and influence there than anywhere else.

No wonder the anarchist Buenaventura Durruti, who in July 1936 was one of the first to organise the resistance against the Francoists and join the Aragon front with a unit of three thousand men, later known as the Durruti Column, was an emblematic figure of the civil war.

No wonder the Spanish Republicans of the first combat section of the Nueve, which escorted General de Gaulle on the Champs-Élysées on 24 August 1944, baptised one of their half-tracks Don Quixote.

All this, dear sir, is entirely your fault.

9

I was talking to you yesterday about Quixote's desire to bring about a world where no human soul would ever be diminished, a happier, more merciful world, a more musical and fraternal world, free of heinous injustice, of selfishness, greed and social contempt.

But, apropos of this last point, I have a new a bone to pick with you, sir: Why do you insist on exaggerating, to the point of caricature, the physical disparity between Don Quixote and Sancho Panza? Is this not a way of reproducing that denigrating logic which claims that social status is seared upon bodies and gestures as if with a branding iron?

Let me explain.

Because he is a hidalgo (*hijo de algo*: that is to say 'someone's son'), you endow Quixote with an emaciated and spiritual face (like yours), a back as upright as his soul (the right physique for the job), and though dressed in the dowdiest possible manner, covered in dust and extremely thin (like a saint in an El Greco painting), he has a look of great majesty. Eccentric, perhaps, but possessed of solemn dignity and noble presence on his mount.

And Sancho, because he hails from the lower classes (i.e. son of no one, son of nothing), is necessarily depicted as bumbling and flabby, obligatorily paunchy, hence his name, which sounds like an offensive nickname; necessarily short, stocky and spindle-legged, obligatorily a glutton and a garlic eater, obligatorily a spouter of crass proverbs, slouched on his donkey's back like a sack of potatoes.

You see, sir, this disparity in general look and carriage, which seems to me related to the way in which you have projected social categories upon the two, upsets me even more than all the rest.

And I say this despite the fact that this contrast between the two – Mr Elegant and Mr Redneck, the string-bean and the fatso, the aristocrat with high-and-mighty ways and the plebeian hick, a simplistic contrast, devoid of nuance, and, to be quite honest, cartoonish – has provided joyous inspiration to many a painter and illustrator.

But I feel bound to make amends, sir, and do you justice.

Because you gradually generate a welcome change. With every page, your view of these two grows free of discriminating logic and social hierarchy. You tear them away from their original status, sometimes to the point where their roles are reversed.

Quixote gradually abandons his pompous and bombastic tone (though it's never pedantic or infatuated), which he believes to be that of knightly heroes, too affected, verbose and emphatic not to be laughable – here is a brief example: *Scarce had the rubicund Apollo spread o'er the vast expanse of the earth the golden threads of his abundant hair* (Quixote talks to himself this way, undoubtedly to practise the convoluted language of knights-errant), *scarce had the little birds of multi-coloured plumage attuned their notes with dulcet and mellifluous harmony to hail the coming of the rosy-fingered Dawn… that the famous knight Don Quixote of La Mancha, etc.*

As I was saying, Quixote gradually abandons his lyrical grandiloquence, while Sancho slowly asserts himself and allows himself to speak of power, liberty, love and death, with a freedom which defies all the conventions of the era.

He goes so far as to mix his cheeky banter with conversations between Quixote and lords of his own rank. He never hesitates to give his point of view, to the great amazement of a witness who exclaims: *I have never seen a squire intervene in a conversation of masters.*

Sancho humbly recognises that it is Don Quixote who educated him, raised him above himself, Quixote who got him to speak, in the fullest, strongest, deepest sense of the word – and you know the power of the word, sir, for you have the arrogance to write.

His example, his confidence, his ascendancy and stormy eloquence (aren't the great passions always eloquent?) encouraged him to take the risk of speaking (of 'becoming a subject', as psychoanalysts would say).

It must be that some of your worship's shrewdness sticks to me, sir. Even the dry and barren land will yield good fruit if you dung and till it; what I mean is that your conversation has been the dung that has fallen on the barren soil of my mind.

The dry land of his mind grew fertile; his mouth, accordingly, opened, and then a sky unfurled before him. Sancho came to speak in a language so 'convoluted' that his wife Teresa could barely understand him and strongly urged him to stay in his rightful place: that of a pickaxe! To which Sancho firmly retorts: he who does not know how to seize happiness when it comes along must not complain when it goes.

On the other hand, now he can abandon himself, in Quixote's company, to high-flown conversations which make him his master's equal (I said his equal, I didn't say his friend), since conversation is only possible between two people of equal dignity (I said of equal dignity, I did not say peers).

Quixote and Sancho move towards each other and confabulate together.

Watch them jogging side by side – sorry, riding along a dirt road side by side beneath a silent sky, exchanging points of view on posterity and glory, themes particularly dear to Quixote's heart.

Sancho, who does not feel compelled to share the opinion of his master as the usual rule would prescribe, roundly declares that as far as he is concerned, the trumpets of fame are foul-mouthed, and that he doesn't care a fig (why a fig?) about public approval and adapts very well to being simply what he is (I am summarising here).

In Don Quixote's eyes, the desire for self-promotion and the pleasure of being admired by the masses (who are always ready to swoon at the feet of yammerers and the loud mouths – parenthesis mine) spurs ambitious men to fatal excess.

However, Don Quixote firmly asserts, to obtain a prestigious title after years of intrigue, calculations, betrayals, solicitations, scholarly shenanigans or infamous sycophancy, practices grouped together nowadays under the name of careerism, seems to him quite miserable.

According to him, there is no other glory than that which is virtuous.

And he would not, for anything in the world, want prestige that is as ill-gotten as it is ephemeral!

So he abandons it to the mediocre beings who work tirelessly all their lives to ensure they have acquired a little propaganda and related advantages (money in proportionate quantity and – very important; indeed, more and more so – the narcissistic display, through all possible means, of their ever so precious and irresistible person – I'm laying it on thick), a propaganda which, in this world so quick to forget, will fade like all the rest.

Quixote, on the other hand, will content himself with Glory in future centuries, a Glory that extends to the entire Universe, and is even, if possible, Eternal.

In other words: there are no guarantees.

Day by day, as I was saying, the bond between the two men flourishes, as trees grow, as friendship germinates. And they will end up forming an inseparable twosome.

You treacherously imply, sir, that this twosome constitutes something which psychiatrists call a case of 'folie à deux'.

That is because you don't know (and this saddens me) what true meeting is, the meeting of two beings.

It is because you don't know what friendship

is, sir, the kind of friendship that can only exist in the most perfect equality and the most benevolent respect for disagreement and dissimilarity; friendship which thwarts all perverse effects of domination and dismisses the violence of a world where each is driven to subdue his fellows by all possible means.

It is because you don't know what faithful friendship is, tenacious friendship, unique friendship between two men who, together, due to – or rather thanks to – their contrapuntal differences (I use the word for its beauty), achieve a combination, a most harmonious arrangement, a duet as one would say in music, an attachment, a complementarity, a rapport: unfailing and irrefutable.

A balanced duo, sir. A *sol y sombra* twosome, as they say back home. I have just discovered that Sol y Sombra is the name of a drink that is very popular in your country, a blend of sweet anise and rocket fuel. This corresponds to our duo, absolutely.

A balanced duo, sir, but almost too perfect in its contrasts and its oppositions – almost too perfectly complementary to be believed.

Could it be this ideal symmetry that has made it legendary?

Because I'm happy to tell you, sir, your ideal duo has indeed become a legend. Would you have suspected in your lifetime that your two creatures would survive and have such a beautiful future?

I guess that makes you rejoice. But let me tell you, you who treat them so shoddily, though you no doubt love them as much as you hate them: you don't deserve them!

In any case, those two escaped you a long time ago and have been living their own lives for four centuries – beyond your control and quite independently.

Since then, it even seems they have gained power, density and glory.

10

The duo you created, sir, has become the stuff of legend – you left this world too soon to know it. And now I will try to give you the reasons for this propensity for becoming legend, which you probably did not at all foresee and which asserted itself slowly over the four centuries that stand between us.

One is endowed with a ruggedly sound sense of reality.

The other has inextricable and incessant run-ins with reality.

One has his feet on the ground (and often in the mud).

The other makes his way through mountains and forests without ever taking his eyes from the stars; and when he arrives at a peak, it is the sky above that he desires.

One struggles at the most trivial tasks: keeping a roof over his head and food on the table (poorly), controlling the purse strings, caring for the animals, smoothing rough edges that could cut and scrape

– in other words, taking care of base material considerations and their waste waters.

The other cannot limit his existence to the sole concern of living, and endlessly gallops after the 'inaccessible azure of Mystic Heaven'.

One (Quixote) is choleric as well as good, infinitely, incurably good.

But don't imagine for a moment that his rages are quaint little fits of pique, wee surges of heat, tiny temper tantrums, the rants of a curmudgeon whose only aim is to reassure himself about his manly prowess.

His anger has nothing to do with the foot stomping of a short-tempered crank, or the short-lived eruptions of overworked temperamental types, nor with fits of hysterics, or the fulminations of amateurs who scream 'arsehole!' in their cars, heard by no one. His rages are grandiose – Homeric, colossal rages, upper-case rages of those, and only those, who change the world because all the stray, drifting anger of their times has become concentrated in them, sometimes without their knowing. Rages equal in fury to those of Ariosto's Orlando, of whose exploits Quixote had no doubt read before he turned into a knight-errant.

The other urges Quixote to be patient, calmly tries to keep his rage bridled, and proves to give excellent advice on how to prevent it from flaring up.

One of the two, who has nothing but contempt for danger, charges headlong at all obstacles. Lightning. Howling winds. The mighty gale that blows the mast down. The sublime moment. Then wham! Reality. The other reasonably weighs the pros and cons – the latter, above all. He contrives to curb his foaming lord, to temper his combative ardour, whispering: *to withdraw is not to flee; and it is not reasonable to wait when the danger is so great that there is no hope at all* – which is Spinoza, through and through! The virtue of a free man, Spinoza says, shows itself to be just as great when he avoids danger as when he triumphs over it.

He flies to his master's rescue when he is in dire straights or headed for disaster, which is often. On more than one occasion, his common sense saves his master's skin, to the point that we no longer know if it's the lord or the squire who holds the reins.

For example, Sancho begs him to forego taking on two lions – immense and famished – being transported to Madrid by ox cart in a cage, gifts to his Majesty from the Governor of Oran.

For Quixote, who wants to prove to himself and others that he trembles before nothing and no one, and that with his halberd he can take down the wildest beasts, calls in a most threatening tone to the keeper of the peculiar crew:

Come, scoundrel! If you don't open the cages this very instant, I'll pin you to your cart with my lance! Sancho begs him in tears to give up such madness, next to which the adventure of the windmills was small potatoes.

But Quixote remains deaf to these entreaties. He leaps from his horse, fearlessly draws his sword, and goes boldly to stand before the cage whose door now stands ajar.

The lion, indifferent, opens a huge mouth, stretches with ease, yawns at length, looks from one side to the other, and then turns his back on Quixote and presents his derriere.

A waggish end to the episode.

One is like my dear Marina Tsvetaeva, a Russian poetess whom you would think crazy for sure, and who said of herself that she was excess in a world of measure – *hubris* in the Greek language, the *hubris* of which Alcibiades accused Socrates, which made him prone to insolence and outrageous behaviour; 'Socrates, you are passing the limit!'

Quixote passes the limit.

Quixote is excess in person.

Quixote is excessive in everything he does.

He is excessive in love and never haggles over its cost, for the very good reason that love is infinite or not at all; for the good reason that a stingy, rationed love is not love, but its aping.

Nor does he haggle over his moral standards, for the good reason that these by definition tolerate no reservations or concessions, and require tireless effort.

He has nothing in his character of the shopkeeper's parsimony that sordidly doses, weighs and reweighs, counts and recounts, quibbles, nitpicks over a few piddling coins and lives in fear of passing the limit.

Quixote, on the other hand, pushes the limits further with each advance. And that is when he does not overstep or overturn them.

The other one (Sancho) has a sense of measure – an eminently French virtue, so they say, and the object of great national satisfaction, excess being left to the Spaniards and other flashy foreigners. A convinced Thomist, without being aware of it, he uses the sense of moderation he is known for to reconcile his faith with his reason, showing a slight preference for the latter when it makes a timely decision involving his wallet.

One firmly believes in his cause, which is to rid the country of villainous rabble, whose numbers were considerable, it seems, in Spain at that time. And I who address you from another world, sir, believe it too.

When I'm having a good day.

The other is much more sceptical about the success of such a vast undertaking.

One believes in evil spells and enchantments each time an event occurs whose meaning he cannot grasp (curses and enchantments are to your time what conspiracy theories are to ours).

The other is endowed with unsparing common sense. My neighbour Marcelin would say it, 'No flies on him', that one has his head screwed on right, and no one's leading that one *down the primrose path*. He won't mistake the moon for green cheese, or a flock of sheep for soldiers lying in wait! He's not the kind of sucker who'll buy a story like the world is *blue as an orange*. I mean, seriously?

But no matter how wily he is, at times he is infected by his master's exaltation, his conviction and dazzling flashes of madness. And if he is often frightened by Quixote's actions and sometimes flees, fearing they will be his undoing, and if some days it occurs to him that they lead nowhere, at the same time, he is dazzled by their panache and infinitely beguiled.

In the grips of a delicious anguish, Sancho, at once desiring and fearful, ends up surrendering to his master's pipe dreams, and lets himself be carried away, subjugated and bewildered, down the fevered paths of the imagination. The phenomenon, known to science by the name of 'quixotification by association', is one by which I am seriously afflicted, sir.

And then Sancho catches himself 'adorning and fantasticating'.

He wishes to possess the same greatness as that of which he is the bedazzled witness; he dreams aloud of power, opulence, glittering things and high-sounding names such as 'Your Lordship'. He even comes to be persuaded, on the basis of a promise Don Quixote dangles in front of his nose, that one day he will be governor of an island (whose only drawback, he says, is that no one knows where it is), and that his wife Teresa will ride in a carriage (because for the wife of a powerful man to go on foot is like walking on all fours), and his daughter, endowed with the title of countess, will be hoisted on a pedestal lined with more velvet cushions than all the Almohades of Morocco ever had in their family (I am quoting).

One of the two is good, fundamentally good, absolutely, infinitely good, I can't say it often enough, good with the goodness of saints, good with a goodness that does not even bother to appear so, and which arms itself and attacks when it believes it has been desecrated.

Good with an open goodness, tirelessly open, tirelessly welcoming, which allows Quixote to see Maritornes, the servant at the inn, not as the strumpet she is in the eyes of others, but as a young woman with such a charitable soul that she gives herself so as not to let men consume themselves in torment.

Beneath his martial exterior, Quixote has the most loving, most compassionate heart that ever was. The most tender too. Rump steak.

And his clumsy tenderness, his rogue benevolence, his overwhelming humanity, is most of all expressed in his bond with Sancho (whom he sometimes rebuffs because he is immensely electric and emotional, but to whom he immediately apologises for his outbursts).

He never makes a pact with anyone against Sancho.

He never betrays him.

He never dissociates himself from him.

For example, he violently refuses to join the morons who pushed his unfortunate squire into a blanket and threw him into the air like a poor ball.

Indeed, these jolly fellows found nothing more amusing than doing to Sancho what people did with dogs during Shrovetide. *The cries of the poor blanketed wretch were so loud that they reached his master's ears. So from the back of his horse he began to utter such maledictions as it would be impossible to write them down here.*

This miserable spectacle, says Quixote, gave him more pain in his spirit than Sancho had in his body.

To spit on friendship, to collude at the expense of a man who has been taken in, to laugh in a pack before a man who is being belittled and whom we are causing to suffer, is not Quixote's style!

The hidalgo's joys are harmless. The performance of somersaults, naked from the waist down, which exposed such things that Sancho went off without waiting to see any more is enough to make him happy. Enough for us, too, sir.

Admit it, then: this childishness is less offensive to the eye (and the soul) than the monstrous selfishness of dukes and duchesses who, to satisfy their little whims, play with their subjects like puppets.

According to Sancho, who knows him best: Not only has he no thought of doing harm to anyone, but only good to all, nor any malice whatever, but a child might persuade him that it is night at noonday; and for this simplicity I love him as the core of my heart, and I can't bring myself to leave him, in spite of the foolish things he does.

But although he is incorrigibly good, it does not mean our hidalgo is a paragon of virtue.

As soon as anger takes hold of him, he bristles, with a look of fury in his eyes. He fidgets in his saddle, grows peevish, flares up like a torch and begins to swear like a carter. I should have just said 'like a Spaniard', for the Spaniards are the uncontested kings of insults as long as your arm: *me cago en la puta madre que te parió*, to name only the most classic of them.

He is excessive, as I said before. Everything about him is over the top: his stormy way of speaking, his thirst for justice, his fantasised love, his pride and probity, his valour, his inflexible will and overdeveloped sense of honour.

He is spirited. Always ready to bolt, like a wild horse.

And at the same time he is distinguished. Always very distinguished.

Even when hurling abuse at his adversaries and fulminating.

With the occasional hint of arrogance possessed by those who have a just awareness of their own worth.

Super quick. As if who-knows-what sense of

urgency were driving him to make haste, as if he were forever behind schedule in life and had to catch up at all costs.

Probably aware that his days are numbered and that he must hurry to get started before it's too late.

So eager to move forward and act that he forces things to happen, he provokes them – and that is when he does not invent them from scratch.

Inopportune, because he is passionate, driven by a vital impulse that often overpowers him, overflows the boundaries of his being, whose strength and abundance he lavishly dispenses to everyone around him; a vital impulse which can violently erupt when his inner immunity is chafed by too many intrusions.

The other (Sancho) is, let us say, a good egg, a good sort, the best man on earth, says Don Quixote. And it's true that he shows Quixote a touching solicitude, absolute devotion. He is considerate without being servile, he coddles him with meticulous care, helps him to put on his clothing, urges him to eat when he forgets the need to do so (once he has launched into an oration as long and convoluted as it is abstract, as is his wont), protects him against others and even more against himself, instructs him on practical matters with which his master struggles in a comic fashion (when he gets tangled in his stirrups, he is

Buster Keaton at his best), makes him pull up his boot straps – in the psychological sense – when he starts to rave, tries everything possible to bail him out of the most inextricable situations, cools him down when he is boiling over, and moderates his outbursts when he sees him heading for a brick wall.

If he ever lies to him, it is out of delicacy, so as not to offend his highly sensitive nature. For Quixote tends to bursts into flames when he feels that aspersions have been cast upon his honour, which happens almost every day that dawns (let us not forget that he is an Iberian, and any self-respecting Iberian must be very sensitive to the question of honour, or change country).

But Sancho is not always well-disposed towards his master. Sometimes after having uttered close to one hundred and twenty curses silently addressed to the one who drags him into such insane predicaments, he is visited by the desire to send him packing with no further ado: his crazy capers are too crazy, dead ends that cause him to suffer from thirst and even more from hunger, force him to rough it, sleep on the ground, endure inclement weather, and puts them in real danger of ruin.

Sometimes he behaves cruelly towards Quixote to get him off his back, for example, making him believe he has indeed delivered his love letter to the Lady of his heart, or having him kneel before a fake Dulcinea with a puffy face and snub nose whom he claims to be the victim of enchantment (today we would say the victim of a spell).

Worse, one day when Don Quixote is about to whip him, out of an obsessive desire to 'disenchant' Dulcinea (in his fevered mind, whipping Sancho and disenchanting Dulcinea somehow go hand in hand), Sancho trips him up and tackles him to the ground, his knee pressed against his chest.

Traitor! gasps Quixote, how dare you revolt against your lord and master? How dare you attack the one who breaks bread with you?

Sancho's masterful reply:

I attack no one. And I am master of myself…

One (Quixote) is a migratory bird 'exiled to the ground, amidst a jeering crowd'. A foreigner.

A foreigner who stands out in the Kingdom of Spain which, at that time, was as closely supervised as a penal colony.

A foreigner with no other country but the one inside, who muddles along as best he can in a forest of signs he interprets in his own way, often askew.

A stranger who does not speak the idiom of Everyman, but a literary tongue that almost no one understands.

Who is often completely off base, his actions inappropriate in the face of the established order, and almost always to his own disadvantage – the exact opposite of the opportunist, who is always exactly where the cameras are.

Who is delirious in the literal sense (etymologically, delirious is 'to deviate from the furrow').

And who shows the world the face of a stray, his innocent and poorly contained soul written all over it, lighting it up with a tremulous glow. The perfect counter-example of the guy who is proud of his pedigree: hunter's garb, belligerent swagger, and forward-thrust accusing chin.

Misunderstood by the times in which he lives, lonely, unwelcome, or downright excluded by people who think themselves reasonable, Quixote endures the fate of all those who – too soon – reveal a few facets of truth about the society in which they wander. Because only *Time reveals all, will tell the tale when we least expect it*, the wise and prophetic Don Quixote confides to Sancho Panza.

The other, by contrast, is perfectly well-adjusted, as we would say today, with a wife, daughter, and an affectionate donkey, probably a little packet of money under his mattress, a little farm, a little patch of land, and a little herd of nimble and capricious goats.

He could be a nice big down-home peasant

bumpkin, a good father and husband, a bon vivant, good guy, middle class, centre-right, sympathetic and crafty.

A nice big oaf of a peasant who is nobody's fool. He knows the devil never sleeps, and that there is no obligation to slay all those who deserve it, since we live in a far from perfect world, or as your contemporary, François de Sales, would say: man will do what man will do.

A big wily, thoughtful peasant, whom the incurable other-worldliness of his master and his ignorance of 'what man will do' regularly make him fear the worst.

One is as candid as anyone can be, and the first clever Dick who comes along can take advantage of him. But if he is more candid than the average, blind to the trickery and malice of men, it is because he is simply not capable of imagining such things. It is because his soul is innocent. Don Quixote is a perfect innocent. Don Quixote is a dangerously innocent innocent. Pure of heart. A child.

But thanks to who-knows-what saving grace, he has been able to keep the child in himself alive – the mark of a poet, so they say – and retained a love of childish pleasures.

The other tries to open his eyes, sometimes none too gently. When, for example, Quixote asks him about rumours going around about him, Sancho tells him point blank that common people take him for a madman, gentlemen for an impostor (does a hidalgo wear black stockings mended with green silk?) and knights-errant for an interloper. The message is clear.

And after Quixote has descended into the cave of Montesinos where he claims to have seen wonders galore, Sancho tells it to him straight, tells him that it is all stuff and nonsense, tall tales, and that in short, he is showing off, even if you kill me for what I have just said. The truth for Sancho is non-negotiable!

Sancho is cash only.

He says things with no frills or carefully phrased remarks.

He is the friend everyone dreams of having.

He does not know how to hold back what is on the tip of his tongue, which tends to be sharp, and which Don Quixote always fears he will unbutton in the presence of prissy people and delicate ears. He loves sayings that are well-chosen though of questionable taste, and raises his voice whenever he deems it necessary. It takes more than the presence of a duke and a duchess to make him button his lip! Distinguished villains don't impress him (or not for long!). He has his dignity, he has his own self, and no one in the world is going to trample him underfoot! Let them put a finger in my mouth, they'll see if I can bite or not! he announces boastfully. Blusters?

A Freudian before his time, he attributes great importance to speech: Keep your mouth shut, as if you were mute, and never dare to say what is in your heart.

One has the pride of a child. Or a toreador.

And a certain penchant for braggadocio and boasting.

Because I must grudgingly acknowledge that Quixote is often caught blowing his own horn. He likes to show off, boast, put on airs – this is his vanity. He doesn't exactly hide his light under a bushel; he thinks he's the cat's meow, Sancho would say, and he likes to be flattered accordingly, especially by ladies (though he expects no favours from them, I hasten to add – he has no intention of trying it on), just to satisfy his pride in the most puerile fashion.

He's a tad megalomaniac and overestimates his strength, overvalues himself, to use the expression of our financiers, whose vocabulary is slowly infecting our language – a scourge, dear sir, a scourge you were lucky to escape.

He wants to make the literary word flesh, *nada menos*; he believes himself absolutely invincible; he imagines himself destined for the peaks where eagles nest; conceitedly, he claims to be able to singlehandedly undermine a column of one hundred Turks; declares that he is equal to an entire army on his own; ready to face the devil in person; imagines that he's a hit with young girls and no one can lay eyes on him without falling in love. For good measure, he asserts that if his vocation as a knight-errant did not absorb him so completely, there would be nothing he could not do, no object he could not manufacture, *especially when it comes to birdcages and toothpicks* (as you have him say with your customary wit).

Imbued with what some have called delusions of grandeur, Quixote strives to present an idealised image of his person, valiant, sublime, and theatrical, an image of omnipotence with which he identifies, and of which – truth to tell – he is a prisoner.

Indeed, it is his fatal flaw, the desire to vanish into the image he creates of himself, merge with it, meet the standard it sets. Fortunately, he never meets this standard, which is a death trap.

Therefore, if one is somewhat immodest and takes himself for the embodiment of a chivalrous hero, the other is humble, provident, balanced, prudent (almost cunning), and good-natured. There is something solid and fatalistic about him. *No friend to strife and quarrels, and useless in a brawl,* but on the other hand he can imitate to perfection the long and painful braying of donkeys.

In short, he is the opposite of the hero as we imagine him. Has anyone ever heard Achilles – or Perceval le Gallois – bray?

However, he is extremely sensitive to the show-off side of his master, who is endowed with a sublime heart and passionate soul, speaks Latin as perfectly as a Bachelor of Arts, knows all the laws of distributive and commutative justice, displays an eager courtesy, especially to the fairer sex, talks like a book, that is, spinning out his words, making the gravy go a deliciously long way, and deploying in the face of adversity a most astounding courage.

To say that he admires him is an understatement.

And in his admiration, he goes so far as to compare him to Saint James the Moor-slayer, a character raised to the ranks of national hero for a long time in Spain, having topped a substantial number of Moors in 844 (whence his legendary name) in the Battle of Clavijo against the army of Abd el-Rahman II but, in recent times, subject to controversy.

One possesses great courage (heaven knows I've said it often enough), disdains his own interests, and wants nothing to do with death – the horizon we all share, which establishes our limits. Therein lies his strength, therein lies his weakness. And, in the eyes of some, his madness.

But if it is true that Death strikes men with terror, staggers their minds, or precipitates them into the most imbecilic amusements, and if it's true that the fear of dying basically prevents us from living, Quixote appears to have sensed that the best way to overcome this fear is not to ignore or deny it, but to face it with eyes wide open, stand up to it without blowing it out of proportion.

Sancho does not share his lord and master's way of seeing things. A *corazón de mantequilla*, he sometimes bolts at the first sign of danger (while alleging compelling reasons for doing so). He takes advantage of the general chaos to hide behind a tree in terror; he trembles from head to foot, as if from epilepsy, when the situation turns to disaster; he crosses himself fifteen times in a row and at top speed while praying to the Lord (the Other, the All-Powerful, the Man Upstairs) to save them. When fear takes hold of him, he succumbs, irrepressibly, to fits of colic, which twist his guts in knots. Once he is even driven by a terrible fright to climb like a monkey to the top of a tree.

Sancho has an astonishing aptitude for life, for friendship, pleasure, good food, grandiose dreams… And for him, no cause in the world is worth dying for and depriving ourselves of all these things.

One is radical; I will not mention this again.

The other is gifted with the art of compromise which Quixote is completely lacking. As soon as he sees he is cornered, he gives way, lies low, retreats willy-nilly, cautiously obeys, makes concessions and ends up philosophically accepting his human limits.

Sancho knows how to make the best of a bad job.

He is the man of the middle of the road.

A man of arrangements and renunciations.

And to surrender (so say those who possess a passion for surrender) one needs courage, another form of courage than that of Quixote. A less sensational, less hair-raising, less show-offy, less orgasmic courage; a pallid, nerdy courage, a modest courage if such a thing can be conceived.

A courage which instead of making you greater, diminishes you, makes you smaller, and leads you to accept blows, opprobrium or debasement, to accept the unacceptable.

But can this really be called courage? Can true courage be satisfied with such diminishment? Allow me, sir, to doubt it.

Sancho, on the other hand, shows a form of courage worth its name, though it is as dull and devoid of panache as the courage of surrender. His is the courage of fidelity, that is, the stubborn, everyday, unassuming courage, bereft of lyricism or display, that of resisting the temptation to escape, despite hardships past and future, and to persevere in a relationship through thick and thin, in the name of the friendship which consolidates and bolsters it every day.

One is very attached to his skinny nag.

The other loves his donkey almost as much as he loves his wife, calls him his friend and companion in misery, and cries his heart out when it is stolen. He also declares he is hostile to hunting (a hobby which he says is reserved for layabouts and idlers) because it is inconceivable to him to kill an animal that has done nothing to him.

Animal rights activists, far ahead of their time! Both show it through the affection that binds them to their quadrupeds, the attentive care they constantly lavish on them, the tender slaps on the rump they reward them with, the overwhelming sorrow they feel when momentarily separated from them, or when one of the two (Rocinante in this case) leaves to go frolic with the ladies – mares – without the permission of his master (which, incidentally, earns him a fine beating from heartless muleteers).

Better yet, among the wonders you relate in your book is the beautiful bond between Rocinante and Sancho's donkey, a bond so tender, so pure and chaste – yes, chaste, contrary to the bias that credits donkeys with sexual proclivities as impressive as they are enviable; a bond of affection, a bond of friendship, a more-than-human bond between this pair who hurry to rub against each other the moment they are reunited, and able to stand this way *without moving, gazing thoughtfully at the ground, for three days.*

It is a bond of friendship that men sometimes try to reproduce, you say. *For men have received many lessons from beasts, in all sorts of areas: the clyster from the stork, vomit and gratitude from the dog, watchfulness from the crane, foresight from the ant, modesty from the elephant, and loyalty from the horse.*

It is a similar bond of friendship that slowly develops between Don Quixote and Sancho, which represents many advantages for each.

The advantages for Don Quixote:

Sancho is his right hand man, his trusty helper, the hand that pulls him back from danger, his shelter, his rampart, factotum, confidant and consolation, intercessor and psychoanalyst, coach, confessor, butler, lawyer, agent, referee, valet, stooge, emissary, moderator, guardian angel, crutch, brother in distress and self-sacrificing mother.

Sancho knows the world better than Quixote. Sancho understands, for example, that money runs the show, and that there are basically only two families (today we would say two classes): the haves and the have nots, the two perpetually at war; everything else is complete rubbish. He personally prefers the former, because *to this day, 'Have' comes before 'Know': a donkey covered in gold looks better than a horse with a pack-saddle.* It would seem, dear sir, that this is still the case.

I continue to unfurl the inventory of reasons that have made this duo a universal myth: Sancho urges Quixote back on his feet when he is tired of being raked over the coals, when he is rebuffed and suffering other indignities, and about to surrender to melancholy (Sancho has perhaps guessed that his master's great bravado may be hiding some kind of secret distress). *What the devil is this,* he says, *what weakness is this? Are we here or in France?* (I would like for someone, someday, to explain this remark to me.)

In the eyes of Don Quixote, who knows so little about men for having only leafed through them, Sancho is the one who binds him to the human community.

The one who allows him to say 'we'.

Sancho is the most human of humans.

Sancho is Everyman.

He is you, he is me, he is us.

And nothing that drives us is alien to him.

He is neither angel nor beast, but both angel and

beast. High and low. Loyal and cowardly. Selfish and generous. Tender and cruel. Knows himself to be mortal. Like you, dear sir. Like me. Like us.

And that's because Sancho intimately knows all registers of human imperfection. He is able to cast himself as a consummate moralist and pepper his speeches with sayings and proverbs that are nothing out of the ordinary but which Quixote greets with a smile, as if indulging a child's whims. Commonplaces of the genre: What's bred in the bone will come out in the flesh, or: a bird in the hand is worth two in the bush, or: he who sounds the alarm does not go to the fire. We've certainly heard better. But these sayings, with which we are occasionally barraged by Sancho, are the only way for him to introduce – in a cursory, standard format no doubt despised by people of refined taste – the deep, complex and inexpressible things which secretly stir him.

And finally, if Quixote is an exile, a foreigner, a wanderer, Sancho is the haven where he can lay down his burdens, his dreams and wild hopes all at once.

Sancho is his home, as books had been in the past. As books are for me now.

For Sancho, the bond with Quixote is also a stroke of luck. For keeping company with a hidalgo who dreams only of lofty feelings and sublime purposes, and aspires to anything but a settled existence, reveals to him that another life, that other lives are possible.

By naming him his squire, Don Quixote has indeed wrested him away from a limited and frightfully stay-at-home life, a life without risks, without dash, without surprises, and all laid out ahead of time.

He has wrested him away from handling the spade which makes the hands calloused, from excruciating slowness and evening soup in which the spoon is numbly stirred round and round; from the boredom of marriage, from days that are all the same, and deathly winters.

He gave him the chance of a new beginning, a constant change of scenery, the discovery of squirely graces and a world incommensurate with the tiny territory in which he had hitherto been confined.

He opened up the possibility for Sancho to discover another man within, cast away his narrow image of himself, and above all, above all, to live other lives.

Please note, sir, that in my country you cannot find a teenager who does not know by heart this sentence by a young poet of genius, of whom I have already spoken: 'To each being, several other lives seemed to me due.'

On this last point, your Quixote proves unsurpassable. Because not only does he refuse to hear of a unique, derisory and tiny destiny, but, like 'these ocean men' admired by Hugo, who know how to spin hundreds of lives and express with genius the truth of each, these ocean men you stand among, dear sir, next to Shakespeare, he claims under his own name no fewer than twenty-three:

I know who I am, and I know that I can be not only those whom I have named (Lord Baudoin, Lord Marquis of Mantua and Lord Moor Abencerraje), *but also the twelve Peers of France and the nine illustrious men.*

Not counting the twenty-five from the Round Table, the Phoebus, the Belianis, the Tablants, Olivants, Tirants and a few others who must be resuscitated.

That is, Quixote and Sancho form a multitudinous couple, which clearly nothing can divide.

With time and trials, joys, disappointments and annoyances made lighter because they are shared, each won the other's esteem, became indispensable to the other.

In the end, they forged a bond of flawless (or almost) affection, fidelity and solidity.

They are basically like two lost children, two children cast into a world of bullies, who support, sustain and watch over each other with affection.

In a universe, sir, where action is no longer sister of the dream, is it mad to want to stay in the enchanted country of childhood and fiercely disdain the realistic 'you musts' advocated by stubby minds?

I therefore sing the praises (because you have understood that the letters I address to you are nothing but praise for them), without hesitation, of your two characters.

Quixote and Sancho form a couple that mirrors us, in a way. The two cohabit inside us. We recognise ourselves as much in one as in the other, depending on the day and our sorrows. Their revolts, impasses, fears and contradictions are, to varying degrees, our own.

Sometimes we go back and forth between them. One day we are smitten with the absolute, and devour the works of Friedrich Wilhelm Joseph von Schelling. The next day, we are taken over by our pots and pans: reality catches us up and ties us down to trivial things. One day we dream of honours, medals and applause, and at nightfall assess their absurd vanity. One day, we open our arms wide to others, and close them in spite after a sleepless night. One day, in a glum mood, we write texts that are bland and polite but which seem to us sensible, only to celebrate – one month later – the wanderings of Quixote, his bravado and tempests, his fervour and extravagance, his lofty fantasies, his magnificent boldness and the Greek fires that he lights everywhere.

Sometimes the two are divorced in us, are even enemies who compete at will. One shoves our nose in the mire of the world (which has a tendency to spread, it seems), while the other sweeps us towards a poetic contemplation of things. One guides us into a gloomy rut secretly desired, while the other drags us into a flurry of gestures as frantic as they are sterile. And these opposing forces clash inside us, collide and tear each other to pieces, sometimes go so far as to devour each other, to commit criminal acts.

Sometimes we are both, together and simultaneously, violently opposite and violently equal, in a tug-of-war, each pulling with the same force.

At such times we no longer know which way to turn; overwhelmed with vertigo, we find ourselves saying yes and no in the same breath; saying I will stay and I will go, I want – I don't want, I love you – I don't love you, I am your master – I am your slave… A leading cause of collisions, of politico-psychological and affective-sexual entanglements (final breakups and immediate reconciliations, door-slamming followed by unexpected embraces, acid missives neutralised on the spot by the delivery of fifty red roses, etc.).

For once, the two are reconciled in us. And that is wisdom. And death?

11

If you will hear me out, sir, I would like to say a few words about Quixote in love, whom you treat with a most detestable, snarky little smile.

For Quixote is in love, excessively in love, religiously in love, says Sancho. His heart is in love all the way to his liver, he adds, not without mischief.

And what does he do to remain that way?

He constantly flees the object of his love and avoids her in a thousand ways, and on a thousand pretexts.

Which means he has understood things perfectly, sir.

He has understood that distance and absence would engender the pull effect that gives love momentum.

He has understood that deprivation and lack wildly heighten desire (the poets of courtly love wrote that such great intensity was generated by unsatisfied desire that the lover and his Lady went into states of shock when, after enduring a thousand waits and prevarications, they brushed each other with the tip of a finger. Sometimes they even passed out).

He also understood that love meant delusions, deceit, blindness, the projection of purely imaginary qualities on the other ('I don't think she'll like me'). Which, in this respect, is similar to a father's love for a child lacking beauty and talent, a love which (I am quoting your prologue) puts a blindfold on him and prevents him from seeing his defects; he is so blinded that he considers the boy's foolishness as gifts of judgment and subtlety, and represents them to his friends as signs of wit and grace.

He understood that to avoid the inevitable fiasco, care had to be taken not to deepen the abyss between delicious illusion – literary, and generally quite comfortable – and unforgiving reality. Dulcinea had to remain a marvellous fiction, a spotless image, a dream in the paradise of dreams.

He understood that love in close proximity, domestic and well regulated, could not long remain on the highest peaks, and would inevitably engender disappointment, bitterness, loud bickering, and all kinds of hassles – something that almost everyone knows and almost everyone denies.

Above all, he understood that love meant sex, and that sex was totalitarian – it vampirised the brain, clouded and tormented it, plunged it into darkness, and in no time, made you topple into the purest illogicality.

He understood that Eros made one stupid.

Sex, the cock = zero.

So no fucking.

No cajoling, no canoodling or any other kind of bill and coo. No gluey lubricity. No emollient expectations or libidinous ravings that end up making you go soft around the edges. No gruelling anxieties when Ladylove is in a snit or demands her mandatory ration of caresses. No participation in the great work of procreation, although it is heartily applauded by the Nation and Our Mother the Church. And no fornicatory routine – ever!

Quixote will grant himself no special dispensation.

And his love for Dulcinea will remain unconsummated, like Dante's for Beatrice.

The call of the flesh and its so-called enchantments, the sexual torments that leave one in tatters, will in no way make him deviate from his path.

He will not be led astray by them.

He will keep them bridled with no shadow of regret and devote his life to the pleasures of the soul that he knows to be less precarious, less fleeting, not to say less expeditious, less dizzying and far less adhesive, or may I say less hot and sticky, than the carnal kind.

But how can you resist so-called impure thoughts, subterranean desires that torment the body? How to resist the irresistible? How to suppress the ardour over which neither will nor morality hold any sway? Today it is difficult not to see, in the fiery actions of our Illustrious One so many releases of libidinal energy, or ejaculations in the streams of insults that regularly gush from his mouth. But you wrote your novel before 1604, dear sir. Freud, of whom I spoke to you earlier, was not yet born, psychoanalysis had not yet come crashing down on people's minds, and sex not really entered (if I dare use the word) their vocabulary and consciousness. Quixote can therefore enjoy his ignorance in complete tranquillity, sublimate his erotic impulses free of worry, convert them into heroic gestures and sappy vows of love, cultivate his prissy old bachelor ways, with no bother about their oedipal nature.

More austere than a Carthusian monk, more ascetic than a Desert Father, you'll never catch him making a dirty joke (he leaves these vulgarities to the picaros). Never a risqué remark or a double-entendre in the style of 'Mignonne, allons voir si la rose'. Never any lustful speculations nor salacious torments interspersed with long sighs or repugnant lamentos.

As for cooing and serenades under the balcony, a deadly bore for everyone: Not on your life!

Quixote is celibate (like Plato, Epictetus, Michelangelo, Leonardo da Vinci, Beethoven, Newton, Hölderlin, Kafka, Van Gogh, Artaud and so many other geniuses), has no plans for marriage, and the desire to perpetuate himself does not occur to him at all.

All his love for Dulcinea has gone to his head, as they say – an erogenous zone if there ever was one – but he is unaware of it, and so much the better.

He enjoys her in thought (psychoanalysts talk about the sublimation of sexual energy), and that is quite enough for him.

But his cerebral love is no less intense for being asexual.

His love possesses him, drives him; it is his blood, his dope, and the sole refuge of his hopes.

His love is a supreme value for him, all other values go along with it. It is the one on which one cannot scrimp, which cannot be measured or negotiated, and which unconditionally prevails in every circumstance.

His love is pure gift, like his plan to redeem the world.

His love is his reason for being, for living and for fighting.

It's his love that wields his arm.

A knight-errant without love is like a tree without leaves or fruit, or a body without a soul.

Without it, his life would be worth nothing, would be a long, pale winter.

His love, moreover, gives him overwhelming energy, a superhuman force, almost divine, which multiplies by one hundred the power of his actions, enough to overturn windmills.

Without the strength she infuses into my arm, I should not have strength enough to kill a fly.

His love is what drives him to passionately defend that of others, to iron out the obstacles that stand between those who love, like Basilio and Quiteria, separated for a time for base financial reasons.

Finally, his love increases tenfold his sense of the marvellous, which enables him to see a castle in an ordinary tavern – four towers, a silver capital, a moat and drawbridge – and his Dulcinea as the marvel of all marvels whose splendour exceeds that of the sun and stars, and in his emaciated, almost crippled nag, a grace superior to that of Alexander's Bucephalus or the Cid's Babiéca.

Sancho also understood this, in his inimitable way:

For love, I have heard say, looks through spectacles that make copper look like gold, poverty like wealth, and beads of sweat like pearls.

This sense of the marvellous with which you endow your Quixote, the 'marvellous normal' as the poet would say, this ability to candidly recognise beauty in beings and see the world with the new eyes of a child each day, is for us a most precious blessing. For we, sir, human beings of the twenty-first century, are deprived of the marvellous (the only tolerable, permissible marvellous is reserved for children between the ages of two and five at Christmas time).

You have understood by now, dear sir, that I am terribly biased, and I tend to endorse your Quixote in all he says and does.

In a word, I'm a fan.

I can even admit that what I feel for him is the stubborn enthusiasm of a sports supporter, minus the howling.

And I, who usually mistrust sexually frustrated beings whom prolonged dissatisfaction renders wicked, acrimonious and stupid, have the firm conviction that his chastity and his lofty idea of love are less the result of sexual avarice, moral rigour or an exalted puritanism than of the part of him governed by human unreason.

Know that Love… bothers with neither measure nor reason. In this way, it resembles death, for it assails palace dungeons and shepherds' cabins alike. And when it takes possession of a soul, the first thing it does is to banish fear and shame from it.

The pure love he has for Dulcinea, against all reason and in defiance of all plausibility, this absolute, undivided love is his madness, his touch of insanity, his inebriation and excessiveness.

But is excessiveness not the very essence of love?

Saint Augustine said that the only measure of love is to love without measure. It is even, he added, this absence of measure that constitutes its measure.

So who, dear sir, is this Dulcinea whom you created just for him, whose charming name derives from the word *dulce* which in French means 'soft' or 'sweet'?

Who is this Dulcinea with the sweet velvety name he constantly invokes and to whom he devotes his prowess and his life?

She is a girl from the country with whom he was once in love, although she never knew it, and of whom he retained a heavenly memory.

Her name is Aldonza Lorenzo and she was a native of El Toboso, a village in La Mancha.

She cannot read or write.

She is robust, tall with big feet, a loud voice, a mannish face and the hint of a moustache, all of which you omitted to point out, dear sir.

Of cheerful temperament, she is always ready to be amused by everything and to laugh uproariously at his jokes, while continuing to vigorously comb the hemp, thresh the wheat with great blows of the flail or sift grain with tireless energy.

They say she has no equal in all of La Mancha for salting pork.

She also takes care of her barnyard, loads bales of hay on her mule while sweating profusely, and exudes certain odours which do not, strictly speaking, resemble the perfumes of Arabia, as Sancho mutinously reminds his master.

But what does it matter to Quixote that his Dulcinea reeks?

Love accepts the other in his or her entirety, and without separating what is pleasant from what is not.

As long as I see her, whether it be over a wall, or at a window, or through the chink of a door, or the grate of a garden! For any beam of the sun of her beauty that strikes my eyes will give light to my reason and strength to my heart, so that I will be unmatched and unequalled in wisdom and valour.

As for her lineage (the Spain of that time was obsessed to the point of delirium by noble ancestry and purity of lineage), Don Quixote makes fun of that too, loud and clear, which is nothing less than scandalous at the time in which he lived.

She is not of the ancient Roman Curtii, Caii, or Scipios, nor of the modern Colonnas or Orsini, nor of the Moncadas or Requesenes of Catalonia, nor yet of the Rebellas or Villanovas of Valencia; Palafoxes, Nuzas, Rocabertis, Corellas, Lunas, Alagones, Urreas, Foces, or Gurreas of Aragon; Cerdas, Manriques, Mendozas, or Guzmans of Castile; Alencastros, Pallas, or Meneses of Portugal, but she is of those of El Toboso of La Mancha, a lineage that though modern, may furnish a source of gentle blood for the most illustrious families of the ages that are to come.

Whatever her ancestors, his Dulcinea is in any case without equal, since he loves her and she is worth as much, in his enamoured eyes, as the noblest princess on earth.

She is the day of his nights.

The true north of his travels.

His lucky star.

His sky, his horizon.

His Blanche-Fleur.

His sweetest of the sweet.

Everything in him comes back to life to tell her that he adores her and that he is her slave.

Watch him throw himself, spear lowered, at a group of Toledan silk merchants because they have not complied with his request to declare Dulcinea's splendour incomparable.

To his passionate eyes, Dulcinea's beauty is infinite.

She sends him into transports of joy.

Her hair is gold, her forehead Elysian fields, her eyebrows two rainbows and her eyes two suns; her cheeks are roses, her lips are coral, her teeth are so many pearls; her neck alabaster, her bosom marble, her hands ivory and white as snow. As for those parts that modesty conceals from human eyes, I can only think and imagine that they brook no comparison, but only praise.

It is all a bit much, as my mother would have said.

But is that a reason to jeer at him, sir, as ironically as you do?

A part of me, I admit, answers: frankly, yes. Yes, this two-bit lyricism is really utterly ridiculous. Yes, Quixote really overdoes it. Yes his amorous tirades are sweet, emphatic, hollow to the point of idiocy and bloated with desperately dull clichés. Yes, his praise is so hyperbolic (all the more so because love is not 'enacted', as a psychoanalyst would say) that it turns into its opposite, and his lyricism, by dint of being bloated and redundant, is nothing more than a bland, nauseating marmalade. The very negation of poetry.

The other part of me (that of the heart) is much less sure of itself but much more benevolent. It notes with joy that, uptight though he is, Don Quixote lovingly evokes the breasts of Dulcinea (a bosom of marble, yes all right, and not of tender flesh, but still!) and evokes just as lovingly what modesty must conceal from human eyes: that is, her arse and her pussy.

That other part of me will go so far as to regret that this quixotic lyricism has, today, been done away with.

Because you are obviously unaware of that, sir, lyricism fell into disuse some time ago. It has been hunted down, its neck wrung. It has been decried, pushed into the background, sacked: old-fashioned, corny and square, ridiculous, completely has-been. We have discredited it, as we have discredited all literary creations that have attempted to deviate from raw reality. (In 2021, you have to have your nose glued to that reality, or to the screen that simulates it, a reality too hideous, miserable and vile to be taken seriously, and I am barely exaggerating.)

And yet is it not precisely lyricism – the lyrical caress – which our music lacks today?

Is it possible that Quixote's lyrical praise of Dulcinea's dazzling beauty, however outrageous or cliché-stuffed that praise may be, is a subtle way of telling us that all faces are beautiful? All, without exception? That every single one is worthy of awe, the loved one's all the more so? And that no metaphor has the eloquence to give a face the praise it deserves?

Is this not a roundabout way of reminding us that all the lilies of the field, the pompom roses, Chinese carnations, myrtles, camellias, hyacinths, amaranths, creamy milk, organic honey, alabaster, opal, coral, ivory, marble, porphyry, diamonds, rubies, turquoises, topazes, lapis lazuli and all the jewellery of Tiffany and Van Cleef & Arpels combined will never, ever, ever be enough to describe the beauty of a face, because, precisely, this beauty far exceeds the limits of our meagre words?

Is it not a way to quietly inform us that when we declare a woman's face ugly (men, we know, have permission to be unattractive, so no one cares about their ugliness), when we declare a woman's face ugly because it is made of pudgy dough, or has mismatched features, or is spoiled by an insolent wart or a few runaway hairs on the chin, or made up in a way that is ill-defined and violently gaudy, or because of who-knows-what kind of faulty workmanship, we are simply victims of our narrow-mindedness, of aesthetic prejudice, or the latest fashion and the advertising that promotes it; victims, above all, of the inadequacy of words, their failure to portray with subtlety and poetry a face and the thousand different shadings of the soul which throbs beneath it (yes, I use the word 'soul' despite its obsolescence, and there's no way I'm going to apologise for it), the failure to restore the emotion which its presence causes to be born in our little hearts.

In his *Introduction to the Discourse on the Paucity of Reality*, Breton, taking up Locke's ideas on the imperfection of language, raises this central question: Doesn't the mediocrity of our universe stem from our power of enunciation?

And since I have reached a point where I am quoting again, I cannot resist the pleasure of reporting the words of my neighbour Juliette, who, the day before yesterday, told me while scratching her head that beauty with a capital B was almost always 'poorly rendered'. I agree with her a thousand times over. Beauty and love are difficult to capture. They stutter, they murmur, sigh and sing to each other, exude each other's fragrance, shout to each other, or do not say, something that only poetry is sometimes able to restore, to our great consolation. But enough of these banalities, rehashed a thousand times! Let us return to the lyrical matters in hand.

Although he has kept company with literature, our hidalgo lacks words that are sufficiently just, strong and eloquent to praise the superlative, extraordinary, indescribable beauty of Dulcinea.

Dulcinea, he repeats *ad nauseam*, is beautiful with a beauty without equal. However, he avoids her.

Does it (beauty) make him afraid?

Is it possible that Don Quixote is a runaway, ontologically speaking? His epic, a desperate flight?

Don Quixote wanders the roads of Spain, and I can't help thinking that now, the term 'errant' on which he prides himself makes one think of nothing so much as stray dogs whose extreme thinness, imploring gaze and bewildered look gives one a lump in the throat.

From dawn to dusk Don Quixote goes wandering, going where chance and random events may take him. Totally receptive, heart and soul. Passionately curious about the present moment and driven by the desire to yield to whatever it has to offer. Braced to welcome the unexpected, dangerous if possible, because there is something about danger that thrills him. Coming face to face at the bend of a trail with a monstrous shape. Tromping back and forth, in every direction, across his native La Mancha, which might as well be the entire world, its inhabitants all of humanity. Blazing trails through woods, ranging over hills, visiting castles, staying at inns – in perpetual motion, perpetual flight.

Don Quixote goes wandering, in that bohemian spirit so dear to nineteenth-century artists, never settling, living on a shoestring, but free, free, free, and every day discovering the beauty of the world, its hideousness, its marvels, its dark vast nights and the apparitions they bring.

Might he have sensed that nothing is sadder than a life without an outside, without an elsewhere, without mystery, without anything that bursts its banks, or leads it off the beaten track? Might he have sensed that the only escape, the only salvation lies in taking flight?

In any case, this is what the Hebrews, reduced to slavery, understood, fleeing from Egypt led by Moses.

This is what the slaves of America understood before Abolition.

This is what Rimbaud understood, leaving everything behind at the age of twenty, all the old kneelings and woolly canticles of the poets of Paris, scattering it all to the wind of the open sea.

This is what Rainer Maria Rilke understood – Rilke, that high-end exile, who never ceased to cast off attachment and seek out solitude, all the better to get away to himself, as he said.

This was understood by all those who, like Kerouac, hit the road in the 1960s with the desire to break old shackles, experience other lives, other loves, other ecstasies.

I almost forgot the great wanderers of literature,

Lancelot, Hyperion, Ulysses, Bloom, Malone…

And many others.

And so after radically breaking away from his confined existence, Quixote the errant roams with no fixed destination, no set terms, no ties but the fictitious, and no guide but the wind.

Or better, he extravaganzes.

He is going towards he-knows-not-what, but is always moving forward. This thing he moves towards is all-important, but he doesn't know what it is, nor can he name it.

He 'cervanticises', as Juan Goytisolo would say. And to cervanticise is 'to go off on an adventure with one's head covered with a fragile helmet transformed into a great helm, in the uncertain territory of the unknown. It is also to doubt dogmas and so-called truths, presented as intangible'.

He drifts, as the Situationists would have said in 1968. He drifts like the picaros whose restless tribulations your contemporary Francisco de Quevedo will write in *El Buscón*, one of the most brilliant satirical novels in all of Spanish literature. He drifts like the picaros, I was saying, but without the cunning, trickery and roguishness to which misery often forces them to resort, and without the famous *hidalguía*.

Because we can count on the fingers of one hand the picaros who hail from a good family, such as Alonso Álvarez de Soria, the poet bandit, son of a wealthy Sevillian merchant, who will end up being hanged in 1603, a year before the publication of *Don Quixote of La Mancha.*

For the most part, the picaros are beggars, transients, poor students, wandering priests, or former soldiers of the tercios, living off of swindles, fraud, plunder, and not giving a damn about honour as a virtue, which they consider a rich people thing.

Does Quixote seek to escape from what – usually – firmly anchors men, and sometimes nails them: the nice home where thought calcifies, the domestic gestures, the regulated life, proprietary tastes, little arrangements made with the conscience, sexual desires quietly dulled, the escape through books we fall asleep over, the cosy refuge within a group – party, sect, chapel – and preconceptions that hold it all together: everything that attaches, constrains, oppresses, all that in silence drives one to cowardice, renunciation and lies, in short, everything which fills us with shame the moment we think about it?

Or is he wandering around in the hope of meeting himself? Of joining himself? And of becoming in action what he was in dreams?

Eager to create a life for himself, as they say, rather than to let life have its way with him?

Off in pursuit of an impossible match with the idealised image of himself?

Carried away in a relentless headlong rush?

Perhaps with the intention of spreading, as he goes along, who-knows-what kind of inconsolable suffering?

Errancy, in any case, is his destiny.

When it ends, he dies.

12

Quixote in love wanders in a Spain that you, better than anyone, know, sir, for having gone back and forth across it, from every direction, over a very restless, adventurous and bumpy life.

It is true that in your century, adventure is very much a part of the spirit of the times.

Christopher Columbus has just conquered America, an exploit that all experts, scholars and sages had considered totally utopian and unachievable. Tomatoes from Mexico appeared in the city markets, to everyone's amazement, and Charles V declared that the conquest of the colonies was a great feat of chivalry, which had transformed his kingdom into a real empire.

All these conquests actually succeeded in hoisting Spain to the summit of the world's colonial powers, thanks to the precious metals trade (translation: thanks to looting) and to human trafficking (translation: thanks to slavery). I cannot help adding, with your spirit of mockery, which I try to imitate, that in your era, it is not uncommon to see powerful archbishops showing off their dark-skinned slaves in order to display their power and the fortune associated with it, as a Louis XIV chest of drawers is displayed in a bourgeois living room.

But then the first signs of decline appear, especially at an economic level. And the little hidalgos, like your Quixote, will be the first to pay the price.

As I was saying, sir, you led a most adventurous life, and allow me to present you with a few of its highlights, in case you've lost your memory somewhere along the way.

You come from a family which, without belonging to the titled nobility, includes a few gentlemen. It has been written, though without the slightest proof to support it, that your ancestors on both sides, maternal as well as paternal, were Jewish converts to Christianity, called *marranos* (from the Spanish word *marrano*, which means 'pig').

Your father, a doctor, married Doña Leonor of Cortinas around 1540, and two daughters were born of this union, Doña Andrea and Doña Luisa, then two sons, Rodrigo and yourself.

From childhood, you show a passion for reading which leads you to pick up shreds of paper from the street, you say.

As a young man, you study in Madrid under the benevolent gaze of your master and mentor López de Hoyos, and everyone agrees that you are possessed of a cheerful disposition and an extraordinary imagination.

Then you enter the service of the young and fragrant cardinal Acquaviva, accompanying him to Rome as a *cameriere* (valet). As required by your function, you make sure his bed is impeccably made, his sheets fragrant, and his chamber pot a vessel so clean that one could drink from it. But you quickly tire of a position that is not particularly exalted for the budding writer that you are and enlist as a simple soldier in the Christian troops of the Holy League, united against the infidels.

In 1571, at twenty-four years old, you fight in the famous battle of Lepanto against the Turks. In the middle of a bloody melee, you receive three shots from an arquebus: two in the chest and a third in the left hand, the use of which you permanently lose.

But you said you were proud of this injury that earned you the nickname 'the one-armed man from Lepanto'.

After several military expeditions thanks to which you discover Italy, you make the decision to board a ship for Spain in Naples. But during the crossing, your galley *El Sol* is attacked by Barbaresques (the name given to Muslim pirates who roam the Mediterranean seeking to attack Christian boats), whom I imagine dressed in the style of Johnny Depp in *Pirates of the Caribbean.*

You are captured, taken to Algiers, and handed over as a slave to Bey Dali Mami, called the Boiteux.

You remain a captive for five long years and, like all prisoners, you learn patience. It will take you a great deal of that to write your books, a great deal of patience, sir, and courage even more.

You make four escape attempts worthy of a cloak and dagger novel, and assume entire responsibility for them, to avoid subjecting your comrades in captivity to reprisals. You prefer torture to denunciation. And that, dear sir, is greatly to your credit. You are finally bought back by the Brothers Redeemers and returned to your native land in 1580 to your greatest delight, *for there is no happiness on earth to compare with recovering lost liberty.*

You return to armed service, and during a stay in Portugal form a relationship with a lady from Lisbon who gives you a daughter, Doña Isabel de Saavedra, who remains with you for your whole life.

Between two military campaigns, you fall head over heels in love with Doña Catalina de Salazar y Palacios, for whom you write a pastoral poem, *La Galatea*, which is published in 1584. You marry its heroine the same year.

The pastoral poem does not bring you the fortune of which you dreamed, so you apply for the modest job of commissioner of food (a hateful task which consists of requisitioning provisions in view of an attack on England by the Invincible Armada), and then you work as a business agent in Seville. It is during your stay in that city that you write most of the *Exemplary Novels* published as a collection between the two parts of *Don Quixote.*

Between your marriage and the publication of *Don Quixote*, you go to prison several times. Some imagine that you created the character of Quixote – who, to say the least, appears sceptical of human justice – with the sole intention of taking revenge on him.

Legend has it that you are imprisoned for the first time one day when you are passing through Argamasilla de Alba, that village of La Mancha whose name you don't want to remember, and call out a *piropo* (a complimentary remark, a slightly risqué gallantry) to the mayor's daughter, who is, beyond the shadow of a doubt, a very decent young lady.

It was the wrong move.

You are immediately thrown in prison, victim of the abusive power of a mayor who is exaggeratedly sensitive to everything that might harm his daughter's honourable reputation, or else was centuries ahead of his time (the first hypothesis seems by far the most likely).

But something good comes of it, for in the solitude of that accursed prison, so they say, you begin writing *Don Quixote.*

It is said that writing is almost always born of pain. You probably slipped yours into the character of Don Quixote in order to feel a little less alone, and a little less heartbroken. Please note that I am doing the same thing with these letters I am writing to you, which will never reach you. Moreover, dear sir, I expect no more than the answers that come in dreams.

You face justice a second time when working as the commissioner of commodities; accused of embezzlement, you are arrested. This case pits you against the chapter of Seville, which accuses you of embezzling church property. But you manage to prove your innocence and are quickly released.

A little later, you are again arrested, this time at Castro del Río in the province of Cordoba, for having caused a deficit of 2,641 réals in the coffers, and are thrown in prison for several days. It has become a habit.

You are then assigned to the tax census for the region of Granada, like Zacchaeus in the Bible, a tedious job if ever there was one, in which you feel yourself slowly sinking into the mire.

Not surprisingly, for you are dogged by misfortune. Having deposited your money with a banker who went bankrupt, this time you are imprisoned for debt. But thanks to this painful ordeal, you meet vagabonds, thieves, crooks, criminals, both wannabe and confirmed bandits – all those pariahs despised by society, scrupulously locked up, all of Spain's hidden misery whose experience would electrify your writing and whip its blood.

Then you settle in a poor neighbourhood of Valladolid where you live in modest conditions with your wife, your daughter, your sister and your niece. And in 1604, you publish the first part of *The Ingenious Hidalgo Don Quixote of La Mancha.*

As you feared, your novel when it comes out is greeted with complete indifference. You then get the idea of publishing an anonymous pamphlet with the name *Buscapié*, a joyous satire of your own book. The scheme is a great success. And suddenly there you are, poor, obscure, without a name or a patron, having gone to prison several times, facing unprecedented triumph.

Your secret? Making fun of chivalrous literature and doing away, once and for all, with its sugary sweetness (on which you throw vinegar), and its implausibilities (some of which, as you reveal, border on delirium), and you make all of Spain roar with laughter.

The result is immediate.

Your book is read aloud in squares, markets, towns, villages, hamlets, at fairs, in taverns and farmyards. Everywhere, it captivates, and everywhere, it inspires joy. In the great houses, the knights' pages tear it out of each other's hands and think it's a hoot. The book appeals to the little people and the powerful alike. Legend has it that King Felipe III, seeing a student sitting on a bench with a book in his hands, rolling with laughter, exclaimed: 'Either he is crazy, or he is reading *Don Quixote*.'

Your novel, sir, is the first Spanish bestseller, second only to the Bible. It is a source of immense joy for you.

But you will face new problems in 1605.

A gentleman called Don Gaspar de Ezpeleta is murdered outside your house and you are accused of the crime, but quickly found innocent.

You finally settle in Madrid, protected by the Count of Lemos (in your time, the patronage of a high-ranking lord is indispensable).

In 1613, you publish the *Exemplary Novels*, in 1614 a long poem in tercets, *The Voyage to Parnassus*, and in 1615 the second part of *Quixote*. You die a year later, on April 22, 1616. They say that Shakespeare died on the same day. It is a coincidence that I am always delighted to relate.

Your novel *The Travails of Persiles and Sigismunda* will appear one year after your death.

What works against you in your lifetime, sir, is that you do not belong to the literary seraglio. And your contemporaries discredit you as they did Shakespeare, for he too is denigrated, defamed, and in particular, like you, accused of mixing the burlesque with the tragic. Like you, he suffers from being far ahead of his time.

They consider *Don Quixote of La Mancha* a minor work – what they find most unforgiveable is that it makes people laugh. There are things in a Catholic monarchy that one must not trifle with. Have we ever come upon a priest in the pulpit giggling and telling jokes about Jesus?

Take comfort, sir, for the same intolerance prevails today. There are a number of subjects that it is frowned upon to joke about; and we risk ruining our careers, sometimes even our lives, by going too far in a spirit of mockery. Would you believe me if I told you that cartoonists were murdered in Paris in January 2015 for having published drawings that displayed religious humour?

The highly endorsed Lope de Vega, a friend of your youth who took the world by storm with his comedies, the poets Luis de Góngora, Esteban Manuel de Villegas, along with a few second-rate scribblers, set out to belittle your novel (in which, truth to tell, you fire a few poison arrows in their direction).

They so disdain you, or envy you, or despise you because of their envy (in truth, your outspokenness gets on their nerves) that in 1614, under the pseudonym Alonso Fernández de Avellaneda, a Spanish author who has yet to be identified, takes the liberty of writing a sequel to the adventures of Don Quixote – an author who hides his name and disguises his country as if he had been guilty of some lèse-majesté, you write in the prologue to the second part.

It is nothing less than a crime of usurpation. And this crime gave birth to a novel entirely lacking in the humour that gave your book its charm, sir, a novel featuring a mad, vulgar, mindless Quixote, devoid of nuance and shoddily burlesque, who finally comes to his senses thanks to pious readings: a complete misinterpretation. This version, which unfortunately was translated into French by Lesage, the author of *Gil Blas*, will be long confused with the original in my country.

Suddenly, you hasten to complete your second part, in which you brilliantly integrate the story of the apocryphal novel and thus put a definitive end to the scandalous imposture.

How?

By vigorously involving Don Quixote himself in the narrative. Coming upon two people in an inn, he mentions Avellaneda's hero and exclaims that he and only he is the true Quixote. You cause your hidalgo to change direction at the very last minute in order to put the plagiarist writer on the wrong track. And in case these strategies turn out to be inadequate, a little later, you make him draw up a certificate of authenticity, before a notary, countersigned by his hand.

Thus you settle the score with the cursed Avellaneda, as you settle scores with all those writers *who write and fling books on the world as if they were fritters*, and this you did, I note with admiration, long before literature was reduced to the level of baked goods.

In the same clean sweep, you dispose of:

- the venomous littérateurs who only feel intelligent when slandering, only excel on discovering others' faults, and *have no other pastimes or pleasures than that of criticising others' works*;

- the makers of doggerel for the use of post-pubescent cretins, sweetening their poems with rose petals, gold-shrouded dawns, tender baby birds and other insipidities of the same saccharine genre – *the arrogant ones, each of whom believe that he is the first in the world*;

- and very especially the writers who, in order to add some density to the nothingness of their pages, slather them with a liberal dose of Holy Scripture, adorning them with a little Christian sermon from a sonnet by some eminent personage, or with a quote falsely attributed to the Emperor of Trebizond, or with a Latin verse, borrowed from Horace, for example, *non bene pro toto libertas venditur auro*, to make people think they are scholars, which, nowadays, as you say, is of no small advantage.

I would personally like to add to this charming anthology:

- rebellious authors begging for state scholarships;
- mud-raking biographers;
- television celebrities fallen victim to the demon of writing;
- the mediocre who only believe in ploys, and slip into your pocket their pathetic scribblings, preceded by a letter stained with greasy sycophancy;
- the skillful who romanticise the misfortunes of others (those of migrants being among the most popular, these days) to soften the hearts of their wealthy clientele, who can't get enough of them;

- the beautiful souls who make their honey from a nice little scandal or a bloody news item;

I prefer not to make the list any longer, for fear of finding myself on it.

That incisive pen, that scathing vein in your writing, like so many lightning flashes, enchants me no end, dear sir, as does your truly amazing feminism.

In *Don Quixote de la Mancha*, indeed, you have created the most feminist character imaginable, in the form of Marcela, a young and very proud woman, very beautiful and determined, who has decided to stay in the ultra-misogynist Spain of the kings Felipe, mistress of her destiny.

An exception.

I almost want to say a miracle.

For although she does not avoid or shun the society and conversation of the shepherds, and treats them courteously and kindly, should any one of them come to declare his intention to her, though it be one as proper and holy as that of matrimony, she flings him from her like a catapult.

For Marcela obviously has many admirers who seek her favours (freedom is always so seductive!), but ruthlessly declines their solicitations and rejects their assaults as with a crossbow (translation: she tells them to go fuck themselves).

Among these misguided suitors is a certain Chrysostom who is mad about her.

Poor Chrysostom decides to distance himself from the indifferent Marcela, in the hope that away from her, the virulence of his love will fade. But far from the object of his love, he falls prey to a thousand fears and suspicions. Jealousy ravages his heart. Disappointed hope darkens into melancholy. His torment only worsens, day by day. And after writing an agonising poem (never omit before a suicide caused by heartbreak, to write, all for naught, lines which include the words pain, distress, suffering, misfortune, harrowing sobs, bitter tears, dark inferno, soul pierced through, etc.), he takes his own life.

On the day of the funeral, Marcela, who has a keen sense of staging (or of politics, take your pick), appears, radiant, at the top of the rock at whose foot the grave of Chrysostom is being dug.

To great effect.

She then addresses the audience with the most feminist speech that has ever been pronounced in Spanish memory, in this land of males and super-males, tumescent males with bulging balls, who, for lack of a sword, pack a .22 rifle (lovingly maintained) or use their hands as a battledore, to put their sinful wives back on the straight and narrow (the Spaniards are champions in this matter, statistics confirm it, neck and neck with the French).

Marcela says:

I was born free, and it is to keep my freedom that I have chosen the solitude of the fields. The trees in these woods are my companions, the clear water of streams is my mirror.

It is to these trees and these streams that I communicate my thoughts and offer my beauty. I am this distant fire, this sword held apart. The men that my sight has deceived, I have undeceived them by my words.

And if desires feed on hope, as I have given none to Chrysostom – or to any other – we can say it was his stubbornness that killed him and not my cruelty. And if it is objected to me that his desires were honourable, and that therefore I was bound to yield to them, I will say that when, on this very spot where now his grave is made, he told me of his purity of purpose, I declared to him that mine is to live in perpetual solitude…

And she goes on:

I have, as you know, a personal fortune, and I do not covet the property of others. I have a thirst for freedom and I do not want to be enslaved.

Sir, have you thought long and hard about the words you put in the mouth of a young girl in 1604? Could it have escaped your penetrating insight that they were truly subversive?

I'll write them down again, for my own pleasure: I have an appetite for freedom and I don't want to be enslaved.

Such was Gelasia in *La Galatea*, such is Marcela, who has not read Simone de Beauvoir, or Virginia Woolf, or Hélène Cixous, or Judith Butler...

Such is Marcela whose words explode in a religious silence before the amazed shepherds: single, 'eco' before the term was coined, beautiful, intrepid, indomitable, born free and determined to remain that way, in one of the most macho countries in Europe.

Her speech finished, the beautiful Marcela theatrically turns her back on the audience, and with a magnificent swaying of the behind (I've added that detail) disappears into the thickness of the wood, leaving all the shepherds thunderstruck, including a few who made as if to follow her.

But Quixote immediately advances, full of majesty. With an Olympian gesture, he lays his hand on the hilt of his rapier and, with the seriousness of a French academician, hammers out the following discourse:

Let no one here, whatever his rank and condition, dare to follow the beautiful Marcela, under pain of incurring my fierce indignation. She has proven, by clear and satisfactory arguments that little or no fault is to be found with her for the death of Chrysostom, and also how far she is from yielding to the wishes of any suitor, for which reason that instead of being followed and persecuted, she should rightly be honoured and esteemed by all the good people of the world.

And all the Weinsteins in power better listen up!

Don Quixote, ardent defender of feminism. It is almost beyond belief! I warmly congratulate you, dear sir, for making him take on this fight far ahead of the avant-avant-avant-avant-garde.

I understand you have yourself learned from the best, and that the beautiful woman you have invented from scratch was probably inspired by your mother Leonor, or your aunt María or your sisters Andrea and Luisa, or your natural daughter, all of whom knew how to read and write, it is said; all of them strong, intelligent, resolute and courageous women.

13

I hope you have understood, sir, that my anger and severity towards you are entirely feigned and have a single goal: to express my admiration for you with the requisite decency and restraint.

Because I am dazzled beyond belief by the cunning attention you devote to concealing what you really think, and the ruses you concoct to multiply the viewpoints in order to heighten the powers of your fiction.

At first, you make us believe that the novel's villain is a cowardly author prepared to deny his work, then the transcriber of a manuscript written in Arabic by Cide Hamete Benengeli, from whom Quixote impatiently awaits tidings of himself – a pernicious work, you say; its thinking even worse – and then a scholiast who doubts the work's reliability, and next, a reactive reader who breaks into the plot to introduce details of his own, then an irate writer who corrects the story told by a mediocre plagiarist, and so on, until our heads are spinning. All these games, stratagems, pitfalls, masks and diverse voices that we have knocked ourselves out to comment upon for the last four centuries, make you, sir, the most writerly of writers.

At the same time as I fake my anger (how could I have the impertinence and poor taste to admonish you, who, in one go, from your love of literature, got rid of the old literature and more or less invented the novel), I kiss your feet for having created this most Spanish character, driven by a most Spanish cult of honour, this figure who, if one believes in the existence of national spirit, in and of himself embodies all of Spain (throw those castanets in the fire or leave them for the Japanese tourists); this whimsical, solitary, ingenuous, ingenious, poignant figure, sometimes pathetic but never bitter and often unwittingly funny; this big-hearted figure, irreducible to any model, this creature of innocence who gives us back a little of the spirit of our childhoods; this creature of poetry whose yearning for the impossible remains eternally our own; this alien who in discovering the world, discovers himself; this intrepid being who through his freedom, shows us the depth and breadth of the freedom we lack.

Through his words, you instil a thousand precious truths.

You suggest that in the end, poetry is the only thing that can stand up to the violence and absurdity of the world.

You tell us that the understanding of this world is

acquired as much through dreams as through actions. Better yet, that the power of dreams is entirely capable of subverting that of logic.

You make us understand that it is impossible to exist without the sweet and beguiling illusions men invent to console themselves for living badly. And you let it be inferred that the most tenacious and widespread illusion of all, whose effects are perhaps the most deleterious, is that of believing that we have no illusions.

At the same time, you emphasise the dangers of outrageous idealism, disdainful of the facts, the great misfortune of desire for the absolute and mass identification with idealised figures.

You throw open the question of whether dreams are diminished or reinforced when they connect to reality, and whether we can hope that through some act of grace the two will intertwine some day and make each other grow.

You remind us that appearances can mislead but that it is pointless to look under their skirts: *only God knows whether there be any Dulcinea or not in this world, or whether she is imaginary. These are things the proof of which must not be pushed to extreme lengths.*

You tell us in passing that *by dint of lies and ignorance, these people* (the astrologers who claim to read the future) *bring to nought the marvellous truth of science.* A statement that is all the more resonant today, as the worst kind of scientific falsehoods circulate on the networks and proliferate.

You confirm us in the idea that the most important thing is to fight, fight, fight, whatever the outcome. For the benefits are in the struggle and the strength one draws from it, more than in its results, however trivial.

You make us reconsider madness and imply, without saying it outright, that in this giant asylum the Most Catholic Spain has become, where men are hunted down by the thousands in the name of a fixed idea (in psychiatry, this is called monomaniacal delusion), one that advocates hating thy Jewish or Arab neighbour as thyself, in this giant asylum, as I was saying, the madmen are not who you think.

And at the same time, you raise the question, if there is indeed delusion, is it really more dangerous that the spinelessness of courtiers, the rapacity of the rich, the servility of cowards or inclemency (the word is weak) of the higher clergy?

Finally, you remind us – and I don't know how to thank you – that literature worthy of the name is dangerous, it undermines the prevailing stereotypes (in your case, those of the chivalric romance, which you happily exaggerate to the point of emptying them of all meaning); it shakes up the established morals and every kind of mind police, including the best-intentioned; it stirs our thoughts by infusing them – casually, or with great sound and fury – with ideas that contravene dominant ideas, its name forever inseparable from that of freedom.

Which explains society's fierce determination to put an end to literature; which explains the giant auto-da-fés which remain stamped on your memory, and whose smoke still darkens the sky of Spain. Which explains the obsession of the niece, the governess, the barber and the priest, to burn, for the sake of Don Quixote's soul, the books that opened up a world to him and incited him to leap into the unknown.

Perhaps on this occasion we could ask ourselves if the censorship to which literature has been subject for centuries, and which continues more subtly, discreetly and insidiously today, is not fundamentally just as effective as those spectacular bonfires.

Because the increasingly brutal confrontation between literature and economic imperatives, which would take too long to explain here, seems to result in certain books being condemned to silence while only so-called money-makers are promoted – in other words, those which, on the pretext of appealing to the greatest number, shamelessly cook up plots appealing to the spirit of the age and never shrink from any kind of boot-licking.

On re-reading the above, I tell myself that I risk being accused by more than one person of outrageously exaggerating the current situation and attempting to compare the incomparable. The thing is, sir, your book constantly pushes me towards anachronism and, irresistibly, to rethink the current events of my country.

You tell us so many dark things, disturbing things about your century, taking care to dress them up in the cast-off tropes of comedy so that they pass without incident and frighten no one.

Because you feel it necessary to bait the reader, put a smile on his face, provide him with a batch of things to laugh at, you entertain him very well, and with remarkable verve, I admit.

Because no matter what I said in my first letters, you are gifted with a rare comic genius.

By declaring open war on seriousness, you cast a spell, sir, on all highfalutin gravity and pomp, all artifice that seeks to impress and thoroughly bamboozle naive readers. And all the while, you make fun of the kind of laughter which disdains and humiliates, the kind whose baseness you constantly expose. Yours is a booming laugh that crushes bitter sneers and spiteful mockery more effectively than any sort of speechifying.

You spare no effort, I was saying, to amuse your reader with all sorts of cruelties (and, as you know, readers are greedy for this kind of thing; they love stories where men kill each other, it fills their emptiness and exempts them from thinking), and other adventures, each more whimsical and preposterous than the last.

You put on a great show with Quixote's noble undertakings and his misfortunes, a vast epic, both kitsch and sublime (no wonder Terry Gilliam made a film of it, after a first, perfectly quixotic failure), with plot twists, acrobatic exploits, savage fights, half-assed stampedes, running gags, misunderstandings by the dozen, pranks, burlas, absurdities, booby traps, burlesque punch-ups, unexpected reversals, sound thrashings, etc.

In other words: humour, laughter, blood, brawling and great confusion.

In short, you've written a series of adventures that makes the tragedy of the Cid look like sloppy sentimentality, and Hubert Bonisseur de La Bath, alias OSS 117, look like a wuss.

All the better to administer your sobering potion.

For under cover of laughter and desports, without seeming to do so, you distil some very full-bodied truths.

You make us laugh and philosophise at the same time, dear sir: a rare thing.

And if your reader laughed so hard in 1604 (though he does so a little less today, for reasons it would be fascinating to explore), it is also, perhaps, to conceal the turmoil those truths provoked in him.

Because you talk to him, to the point that it is unbearable, about the relentless, oppressive violence that reigned in the Catholic Spain of King Felipe II and his successor Felipe III.

A feast of violence, sir, a debauchery of appalling torture which made Nabokov say that *Don Quixote of La Mancha* was one of the harshest and most barbarous books that has ever been written. Violence, whose atrocity in scenes of combat, whose savage ferocity, refinement of cruelty and mortifying treatments, which you meticulously, wantonly evoke, page after page, spare no detail of the feast.

Violence levelled against every single word and gesture that contravenes strict Catholic orthodoxy.

The violence of masters towards subordinates, and of subordinates towards each other, violence confirming what the brilliant La Boétie wrote several years before you, that domination not only distorts and corrupts men to the point of making them love their servitude, but at the same time distorts and corrupts the relations between them.

Violence towards inhumanely chained galley slaves.

Horribly degrading violence towards madmen whom we lock up, a misfortune you reserve for Quixote in chapter XLVI of the first part: hands tied, lying on a pile of straw, sequestered like a beast in a mobile cage, and, you say, in such a state that not even his own mother would have recognised him: dry, yellow, gaunt, eyes sunken to the bottom of his brain, unable to move or defend himself or defecate. Because Quixote, you remind us very judiciously on this occasion, feels the need to defecate unlike the marvelous Amadis de Gaule, who is never seized by such scabrous and unseemly desires. (One may remark that the Spaniards are known to approach without the slightest circumlocution or slightest modesty everything related to so-called natural needs, pee pee poo poo, as if they were taking revenge, through these protests of the body, against the religious purity foisted on their souls for time immemorial.)

Religious violence and censorship violence are silently evoked throughout the novel.

Violence against women as exemplified by this historical episode, gleaned during my research, which I relate here because it is wonderfully evocative of the mood that prevails in the world you live in: at the age of fifty-four, King Felipe II, four times married (the fourth time with his niece, whom he had stolen from his son) plans to marry a fifth time, with the barely-fourteen-year-old sister of the late queen. But he sees his plan falling through, because the contender, terrified at the idea of being the object of a purchase, an acquisition, a barter (I don't know what term to use) prefers to be cloistered in a convent of the Poor Clares rather than consent to such a sordid scheme.

Violence prevails at all levels and every register, in all shapes and combinations, ferocious, venomous, limitless violence which no written word, it seems to me, had ever recorded with the same atrocious precision, and which boded very ill for the times ahead.

Violence to which men are so accustomed that they in no way perceive its abjection and reproduce it without even knowing it.

Worse still: the violence they perpetrate on others seems to distract them for a moment from their own sense of powerlessness, and counting for nothing, while awakening deep within them some kind of dreadful lust.

But if your novel is clouded by violence, sir, it is perhaps clouded even more by disillusion, *el desengaño*, which you darkly share with us.

Disillusionment with Quixote's powerlessness to change the world by sheer force of desire.

Disillusionment on perceiving, with each new

adventure, that ignorance is a strength, and violence its ally.

Disillusionment with men in general: liars, perverse, ungrateful, cruel, and predatory, almost all preoccupied with evil, almost all competing with each other in hatred, whether they are the oppressed or the oppressors, the powerful or beggars, sickly or muscle-bound.

And since you are not writing for the watchdogs of the self-righteous, and in no way seek to mollify, or even less to seduce them, you do not hesitate to describe the fierce and desperate resentment to which the most disadvantaged are prey, thus reproducing, consciously or unconsciously, domination they have incorporated into their most private depths as something inevitable (which they sometimes hasten to perpetuate), as God's will. So be it.

This endlessly rehashed hatred of certain humiliated beings, the bitterness of those who, condemned to being nothing but helpless, have only gall for saliva and hatred for comfort. Certain thinkers after your time will give it the name of resentment.

All the vices, Sancho, bring some kind of pleasure with them; but envy brings nothing but irritation, bitterness, and rage.

And this rage to accuse, recriminate and punish, which feeds on condemnation, vindictiveness and unacknowledged jealousies, this disease of the soul, this proliferating cancer, sir, infiltrates the world in which we live today, while the nostalgic memory of revolts carried out in joy, of embracing life in all its colours (from the most tragic to the most joyful) and a clear-sightedness exempt from all acrimony, fades slowly from my memory. Did I dream those ideal revolts?

Weak and strong, farmers and servants, duchesses and peasants, you give voice to the people as a whole. And in this way you draw a great many out of literary invisibility: muleteers, soldiers, barbers, innkeepers, actors, cowherds, goatherds, puppeteers, millers, valets, escaped convicts, argousins, judges, beadles, priests, canons, dukes and duchesses – the infamous as well as the distinguished – and gentlewomen, duennas, pretentious old bags, boors, peasant women, naive young ladies or teases, girls in love, and girls malicious, debauched, feminist, or simpering; girls Moorish by blood but, thank God, Christians in their souls (the Moriscos banished in 1610 and forced to disguise themselves to escape the edict of expulsion), bandits hanged high in trees, scoundrels with hearts of gold… all this variegated, picturesque Spanish humanity dwelling under the Felipes' reign with its prejudice, its cunning, brutality and grotesqueness, or, more rarely, its elegance.

Though you don't provide perfectly exact descriptions and embroider a little, falsify and exaggerate at will, because you are not a notary or a bailiff as far as I know, but indeed a writer, you superbly evoke the dark and heavy climate that prevails in Spain of the Golden Age.

Disappointment, I was saying. But the cruellest of all is the one you wrest upon Quixote himself before death. And although I still have the greatest difficulty in consenting to this finale, although I hate it, curse it and deny it with all my being, although for me it spells absolute defeat for Quixote and at the same time for ourselves, I am forced to accept it.

Allow me to remind you.

Quixote, in the last pages of the novel, is defeated at Barcelona by the Knight of the White Moon – none other than the bachelor Samson Carrasco – who analyses all with intelligence sharply tinged with scepticism. Carrasco, who is worried about Quixote's behaviour, like all his friends and neighbours, finds no other way to bring him home than by challenging him to a singular combat and making him promise that if he loses, he will stay in his village for a whole year without moving.

This, for Quixote, is the defeat that breaks the camel's back.

The coup de grâce.

Back within his own walls (I was going to say in his grave), his body pitiful, his soul run dry, Quixote, you write, is seized with a high fever and takes to his bed, receiving visits from the priest, the barber, and the bachelor Samson Carrasco, while his niece, his governess and Sancho weep in earnest and languish (grief which, we may note, in no way quells the appetite of Sancho, who stuffs himself with undisguised pleasure).

In the last hours he has left to live, Quixote, very dejected, suddenly realises that he has been mistaken all along, and his enterprise was never anything but a senseless whim, a comforting pipe dream, a deception adorned with the flattering plumage of literature.

With an altogether juvenile ardour, he has doggedly tried to graft upon reality the magnificent dream with which chivalric romances had filled his mind. Now Death, which grows ever more pressing and allows no cheating, incites him to view this project which kept him alive and wildly passionate for so long as a mystification designed to mask the ugliness of reality, smoke and mirrors, a consoling decoy, a vain protest buoyed up by two-bit idealism, a comical mutiny which men treat themselves to from time to time (here, I am laying it on thick, out of spite).

Now I see through their absurdities and deceptions (those of chivalric romances), *and it only grieves me that this destruction of my illusions has come so late.*

That dream, so beautiful and vast, had given meaning to his life, enchanted it, opened it up to great adventure, but his efforts to make it real caused him suffering beyond what any human being can endure, and now he abhors that dream (that is the word he uses).

He sees it as dangerous madness.

He flouts and repudiates it.

And he dashes it to pieces at the risk of doing the same to himself.

Darkness is approaching, the final terrible night will soon fall. Quixote calls his friends to his bedside: the priest, the barber and the bachelor Samson Carrasco, and exclaims, to their great surprise, that he is no longer Don Quixote, but the Alonso Quijano they have always known, whose conduct throughout his life earned him the epithet of 'the Good'.

Then he asks to confess his sins, entrusts his soul to God, and has his will drawn up by the notary. He stipulates that Sancho may keep the amount of money he entrusted to him, and his niece Antonia Quijano will inherit his fortune on the express condition that she never marry a reader of those accursed chivalric romances. In front of his gathered relatives, he receives the last rites and, with what remains of his strength, again condemns those books that scandalously deceived him.

Quixote played the game and lost.

Total failure.

Capitulation all the way.

Quixote is foundering, and his dream founders with him. He has nothing left now but a few moments of life devoid of hope.

The time has come for him to die.

And for me, to despair, dear sir.

14

I told you yesterday how greatly I admire the way in which, by viewing your creatures with an ambiguous gaze (often laughing, sometimes maliciously cruel, but almost always benevolent, in spite of appearances, with a secret paternal affection), you are able to instill certain truths much more effectively than you would through a learned and impeccably convincing sermon.

Better still, you succeed against all odds in putting their speech at the same level: the elegant tongue of Quixote (regularly peppered with vehement curses) and the juicy diction of Sancho, who blithely mangles the conventional formulas, and deems disreputable (to quote one example among a thousand) the phrase 'as computed by Ptolemy' spoken by his master: *that's a nice way to talk – putrid Dolly or whatever it is!* The words of your time were divided into classes, some arrogant and posh, others very lowly, good for nothing but for throwing in the sewer. You render them free and equal, sir, and we take great pleasure in savouring a language which, while overturning the prevailing social divisions, delights us by revealing the plurality of its registers.

But your greatest merit in my eyes lies in the fact that you do not avert your gaze from the terrible, you never smooth the dark rough edges of reality, and unflinchingly report on the nocturnal side of man, allowing literature to take a huge leap forward from which we have not yet entirely recovered.

I can't help relating this sentence from one of my favourite writers who owes you a great deal, as he would often say. William Faulkner lived from 1897 to 1962 and was able to find moving words with which to give a voice to idiots, recluses, the ill-born, the fallen, losers, octoroons and all the damned of the State of Mississippi, USA. He writes: 'Literature has the same impact as a match lit in the middle of a field in the middle of the night. The match illuminates relatively little, but it enables us to see how much darkness surrounds it.'

Would it come as a surprise, sir, if I told you that your evocation throughout the novel of this 'surrounding darkness', of the dark waters where men go to slake their thirst and very often drown, seems almost enviable because it is clearly stated, perfectly assumed rather than heavily disguised, ridiculed or shamefully omitted.

I realised this while rereading your book two months ago.

I studied it at twenty because it was on the

curriculum (at the time, I was enrolled in literature at the University of Toulouse), and I paid only scant attention to it.

Today, I reread it passionately. It is always with me. It reveals itself, to my delight, in an entirely new and extraordinarily stimulating light; its movement inside me never ceases to expand, to rebound and set off a thousand reverberations along with entire worlds of thoughts, images and questions.

Since my first reading, almost fifty years have passed – the time it took me to understand – and your book speaks to me from a distance of over four centuries. It now seems obvious that the darkness, ferocity and arid violence you continue to describe are still, again and again, and always, ours.

I know it is easy to render someone speechless with this lazy idea that we can refer the past to the present and spot all sorts of similarities between them, that our history is repetitive and singularly lacking in invention, that nations remain equally cowardly before their current masters, and that wolves remain wolves no matter how much you cajole and caress them.

I therefore reaffirm that for me there is no question of comparing your era with mine at any cost. Your book simply enlightens me about the current events of my time and reveals ('reveal' is the right word because your novel uncovers what was already there) that this monstrous violence you throw in our faces has continued to the present day but is more dressed up than before, more surreptitious, more captious and insinuating, and better at hiding its dirty laundry.

It has even become refined over the years and taken on a hundred different masks, bedecked itself with a hundred different pretexts.

Violence that we were wrong not to thoroughly re-think after the nameless infamy of the Holocaust. Because I'm not sure we will ever be able to pick ourselves up again after that horror.

Colonial violence, long buried and long silenced, but starting, slowly and with difficulty, to be revealed: massacres, spoliation, forced labour, iron restraints, degrading treatment, and worse.

(But here I have been swept away in my writing, without meaning for it to happen, by a line of thought that rushes irrepressibly into the breach of politics. But how else is one to proceed? How do you talk about the heady scent of lilacs when it is not lilacs but anxiety blossoming inside and outside of us? So I will continue my exposé on the brutality of our times, at the risk of raining on your parade, dear sir – you who love to laugh and can see the funny side of everything.)

Violence, as I was saying, against foreigners, Blacks, Arabs, Jews, Roma, queers, transgenders, women, children, madmen, borderlines, the poor… violence consistently denounced and consistently renewed.

Violence inflicted upon all those who are considered useless to the prosperity of capitalism and treated like dogs, or folded into society while we hold our noses because it is them, after all, who keep the system going.

Violence against lunatics – I know the subject quite well: loss of liberty, chemical straitjackets, pills that bring on deathly fatigue, and a feeling of being internally shattered, or painfully absent to oneself.

Legitimised police violence, reinforced and sometimes visibly admired by governments (who are afraid of them), aimed at social violence secreted by these same governments (who are afraid of that, too), one feeding the other, incriminating the other, executing the other, and vice versa. An endless cycle. A vicious circle.

The violence of a new moral order that grows more moralising every day, more aggressive and intransigent, proclaimed by the new crusaders of the Empire of Good, who, at the least deviation, accuse the deviant and severely condemn them.

A form of Inquisition, sir. A modern Inquisition that is thriving, it would seem, in a worrying way; it claims every right for itself, all the better to stifle contrary opinions; an Inquisition that is all the more pernicious for having taken on the countenance of Outraged Virtue.

The violence of the digital, which acts in such a way that the virtual has now replaced the real; the violence of putting the world under surveillance that it facilitates and reinforces; the violence of the many forms of hatred unleashed on its networks; the violence of the tyrannical transparency it imposes, with which men play along in sheer delight, exposing their little private worlds with the blissful immodesty of exhibitionists flaunting their private parts.

The violence of fierce competition dictated by the market and applied, without shame and without limits, to everything, everything, everything.

Trivialised, massive, global violence to which we become inured, as to a diluted poison. So that only overwhelming disasters succeed in moving us. And even then…

In the face of these savage times, we still hope that new Don Quixotes will finally turn their anger against our gods of plaster and open the way for us.

‘New Don Quixotes who turned their anger
Against the gods of plaster and the shadow of statues
There were a few of us, united by those days
To rail at a strange virtue.’

These Don Quixotes exist today, I believe – I want them to, I hope they do. Tiny Don Quixotes, lonely and anonymous, all courage and high forehead, who may one day unite and combine their ardour.

I often think of the waiter at a bar where I was having a drink, who, because he spoke too long with a few seated clients, was roundly scolded by the boss. In the face of this public reproach, the waiter did the following: ceremoniously removed his apron, ceremoniously folded it, ceremoniously set it down on the counter on the other side of which his boss was busying himself, and in a voice loud enough to be heard by all, he said: ‘I’m giving back my apron, sir. Keep the change!’ And, to the amazement of the boss and the customers, he left the bar on his imaginary horse, head high, his face full of pride.

I think of Nelson Mandela who in 1960, with magnificent insolence, took the risk of publicly burning the internal passport that all Blacks in South Africa were forced to carry under penalty of arrest. This gesture will mark the transition to armed struggle against apartheid, the non-violent strategies which had been applied until then having come to nothing.

I think of Tommie Smith, John Carlos and Peter Norman who, on October 17, 1968, during the presentation of the 200-metre medals at the Mexico Olympics, under the noses of officials, raised their black-leather-gloved fists as a sign of solidarity with African Americans in their struggle for civil rights. Tommie Smith and John Carlos would immediately be banned from the Olympic Village and banned from competition in the United States for life. Peter Norman would also suffer considerable ostracism in Australia and never be selected again.

I think of my seventeen-year-old mother who, having left her native Catalonia by foot in January 1939, after days and days of walking in the cold, with a will that never wavered, and alone, made her way to France, a country of which she knew absolutely nothing. Every time I know I'm growing fragile and ready to give up, I summon her grit and determination, the dignity that kept her so upright.

I think of those other daring beings, those knights errant of literature that were Baudelaire, Rimbaud, Nietzsche, Joyce, Faulkner... to name only a few who speak straight to my heart.

15

The whole world, sir, has made Don Quixote its own. Over four centuries, it has continued to celebrate him, sing his praises, I am infinitely happy to say.

The Romantics saw him as a dreamer with his eyes wide open, a poet who spoke the language of the soul;

The realists as an amusing and harmless figurc of unreason;

Scholars as an opportunity to teach perspectivism and other forms of speciousness, provided they were tedious;

Philosophers as a pretext to question the inexhaustible and cavernous question of evil, the relationship between reason and madness, between utopia and pragmatism, between the individual and society;

Linguists as food for thought on the chasm between words and things;

Men of letters saw the fratricidal struggle between poetry – embodied by Quixote – and prose – incarnated by Sancho;

Freudians saw in him the omnipotence of infantile desire;

For lovers of freedom, he was a torchbearer;
For homosexuals, he was a homosexual;
For rebels, he was a standard;
For idealists, a champion;
For exiles, an emblem.

All took him hostage, sought confirmation in him of their theses or beliefs, and more or less carefully, bent him this way and that to fit their needs.

And yours truly does the same.

Those who would have turned their back on him, had they met him in what is called real life, those who would have mocked, booed, hunted or derided him, the cowards who would have run away from him full speed, the sanctimonious, who would have choked on his barbs, the wise who would have taken him for misguided, the prosecutors for an offender, psychiatrists for a schizophrenic, the venomous for a poor sod, the ignorant for an imbecile, the rigid for a screwball… all of them marvelled, or pretended to marvel at Quixote and put him on a pedestal.

The unjust society he fought against, one upheld by a selfish, greedy and intolerant morality whose abuses he yearned to annihilate, wove him a crown of thorns.

That society turned this figure in love with perfection, this angry man, this righter of wrongs engaged in a merciless struggle to amend the world, into a cult figure, a sacred monument, a universal legend.

So as better to redeem the unredeemable?

So as better to shut him up?

Sometimes I wonder if his consecration and constant celebration over four centuries, often planned by bureaucrats sitting in hushed offices, have not dulled his shine, emasculated him, deprived him of his explosive force, obliterated his tireless powers of subversion, and denied the formidable relevance of his rages.

I sometimes wonder, sir, if the glory he has acquired has not, in essence, made him such a harmless character that his adventures can be discussed without causing a scandal in primary schools.

We continue, in fact, to tell children that this very original character mistook simple windmills for fearsome giants, to the children's great amusement. This, moreover, is the only episode of the book that teachers choose to comment on in class, and often the only one that adults retain, which exempts them from reading the entire novel.

In opposition to these hasty, summary or lazy readings, sir, I would like, in the manner of Spinoza (who ranked you higher than Plato), or of Laurence Sterne (who preferred your Quixote to the greatest heroes of Antiquity), or Montesquieu (who said: The Spaniards only have one good book, the one that demonstrated the ridiculousness of all the others), the Schlegel brothers, Schelling, Victor Hugo (who ranked you among the great geniuses, alongside Homer, Dante, Rabelais and Shakespeare), Verlaine, Balzac (who found Quixote sublime), and I quote these authors pell-mell, Flaubert (who knew your book by heart before knowing how to read), Chesterton, Sainte-Beuve (who called it the Bible of humanity), Apollinaire, Nabokov, Turgenev, Dostoevsky (who hailed it as the greatest and saddest of all books), Rubén Dario, Carlos Fuentes, Jorge Enrique, Torrente Ballester, Franz Kafka, Herman Melville, Mark Twain, Dickens, Joyce, Thomas Mann, William Faulkner (who read your book every year), Bergson, José Saramago, Günter Grass, Gabriel García Márquez (who also knew chapters by heart), Miguel de Unamuno, Goytisolo, Borges, Cendrars, Cioran (who called Quixote hysterical), Camus, Aragon, Michel Foucault, Georg Lukács, Julián Ríos, Arrabal, Montherlant, Thomas Pynchon, Michel del Castillo, Le Clézio (who declared that your book was the most inventive in the world), Jean Canavaggio, Salman Rushdie, and so many others, but, hey, no women writers that I know of (it would be intriguing to understand why), I would like, with a loving mauvaise foi of which I am fully aware, to do my part to restore to the character of Quixote his incorrigible kindness, his radical insubordination and his generous courage.

I would also like to say, sir, that Don Quixote is our brother. Our dreaming brother in a brutal world, our insurgent brother in a lethargic world, our rebellious, angry, inconvenient, tumultuous, incandescent brother who says no (a desperate no sometimes), no to unbearable injustice, no to jaded indifference or limp consent to what may, one day, steer us straight into the worst imaginable end.

This brother, dear sir, this pure figure of fiction, this pure poetic figure, grows more necessary and precious to us each day. It is thanks to the breaches Quixote opened in the walls that surround us, Quixote and other cranks of his kind, that our world remains liveable and desirable.

Thank you, Mr Cervantes.

The Ingenious Gentleman Don Quixote of La Mancha (1605, 1615), by Miguel de Cervantes, is quoted from the translation of John Ormsby (source Gutenberg).

Additional bibliography:

Louis Aragon, 'On vient de loin', in *Les Yeux et la Mémoire*, Paris: Gallimard, 1954.

Charles Baudelaire, 'L'Albatros', in *Les Fleurs du mal* (1857), Paris: Gallimard, 1972.

Victor Hugo, 'Réponse à un acte d'accusation', in *Les Contemplations* (1856), Paris: Gallimard, 1973.

Friedrich Nietzsche, *Le Gai Savoir* (1882), in *Œuvres complètes*, vol. 8, trans. Henri Albert, Paris: Mercure de France, 1901.

Arthur Rimbaud, *Une Saison en enfer* (1873), Paris: Gallimard, 1973.

François Villon, 'La Ballade des pendus' (1463), in *Poésies*, Paris: Gallimard, 1973.

Voltaire, 'Lettre à d'Alembert du 7 août 1766', in *Correspondance*, tome VIII, Paris: Gallimard, Bibliothèque de la Pléiade, 1983.

www.ingramcontent.com/pod-product-compliance
Lightning Source LLC
LaVergne TN
LVHW091140080826
845145LV00008B/2204

* 9 7 8 1 7 6 3 6 0 0 9 0 4 *